Hayley shuddered.

She and Byron were temporarily alone with this patient and there was nothing to do now but keep checking his vital signs and await the chopper. They had oxygen and Haemaccel going in, a slower and stronger pulse and better blood pressure. After all the drama of the day, it was oddly peaceful, and she desperately wanted to say something to her lover to seal the moment.

I'm sorry about overreacting the other day. You didn't deserve it. Can we backtrack a bit?

You look gorgeous in blue-gray, with the wind combing your hair.

If I kiss you, will you get some color back into your face and stop looking like you've seen a ghost?

"That shark..." he said at last, before Hayley could find the right words. "I saw it before the chopper even arrived. It was so close to getting that second guy in the water, I could almost smell the blood. Another second, Hayley..."

Dear Reader,

Perhaps you are driving home one evening when you spot a rotating flashing light or hear a siren. Instantly, your pulse quickens—it's human nature. You can't help responding to these signals that there is an emergency somewhere close by.

Heartbeat, romances being published in North America for the first time, brings you the fast-paced kinds of stories that trigger responses to life-and-death situations. The heroes and heroines, whose lives you will share in this exciting series of books, devote themselves to helping others, to saving lives, to *caring*. And while they are devotedly doing what they do best, they manage to fall in love!

Since these books are largely set in the U.K., Australia and New Zealand, and mainly written by authors who reside in those countries, the medical terms originally used may be unfamiliar to North American readers. Because we wanted to ensure that you enjoyed these stories as thoroughly as possible, we've taken a few special measures. Within the stories themselves, we have substituted American terms for British ones we felt would be very unfamiliar to you. And we've also included in these books a short glossary of terms that we've left in the stories, so as not to disturb their authenticity, but that you might wonder about.

So prepare to feel your heart beat a little faster! You're about to experience love when life is on the line!

Yours sincerely,

Marsha Zinberg,
Executive Editor, Harlequin Books

NO
STRINGS
Lilian Darcy

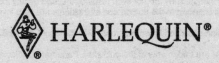

HARLEQUIN®

TORONTO • NEW YORK • LONDON
AMSTERDAM • PARIS • SYDNEY • HAMBURG
STOCKHOLM • ATHENS • TOKYO • MILAN • MADRID
PRAGUE • WARSAW • BUDAPEST • AUCKLAND

ISBN 0-373-51251-1

NO STRINGS

First North American Publication 2003

Visit us at www.eHarlequin.com

Printed in U.S.A.

Lilian Darcy currently lives in Australia's capital with her historian husband and their growing family. They also spend significant amounts of time in the United States. Lilian has written over forty medical romances, and also writes for Silhouette. She loves the Medical Romance line for its drama, its high emotion and its heartwarming tone.

Lilian enjoys travel, quilting, gardening and reading, and is a volunteer with Australia's State Emergency Service. Readers can write to her at P.O. Box 381, Hackensack, NJ 07602, U.S.A. or can e-mail: lildarcy@austarmetro.com.au

GLOSSARY

A and E—accident and emergency department

B and G—bloods and glucose

Consultant—an experienced specialist registrar who is the leader of a medical team; there can be a junior and senior consultant on a team

CVA—cerebrovascular accident

Duty registrar—the doctor on call

FBC—full blood count

Fixator—an external device, similar to a frame, for rigidly holding bones together while they heal

GA—general anesthetic

GCS—the Glasgow Coma Scale, used to determine a patient's level of consciousness

Houseman/house officer—British equivalent of a medical intern or clerk

MI—myocardial infarction

Obs—observations re: pulse, blood pressure, etc.

Registrar/specialist registrar—a doctor who is trained in a particular area of medicine

Resus—room or unit where a patient is taken for resuscitation after cardiac accident

Rostered—scheduled

Rota—rotation

RTA—road traffic accident

Senior House Officer (SHO)—British equivalent of a resident

Theatre—operating room

CHAPTER ONE

AT THE wheel of the ambulance, Hayley Morris turned out of the station driveway into Halifax Street and activated lights and sirens. Beside her, Bruce McDonald consulted the map.

'OK, yeah, it's off Bennett Parade,' he said. 'Beach Road.'

He was a very experienced ambulance officer, though not a fully trained level-five paramedic as Hayley now was. Stocky and grizzled, he could lift a heavy, full-grown man as easily as he could gentle his voice to soothe a child.

Hayley nodded, keeping her eyes on the road. 'I know Beach Road.'

'They've extended it. Maybe this is one of those new houses.'

'We'll soon see.'

It was a Thursday in early February and the town was quiet at just after noon. Another turn brought Hayley to the Princes Highway and she headed north, taking advantage of the wide ribbon of traffic-free grey road to bring the vehicle up to a hundred kilometres per hour. She would go even faster once she was out of Arden.

Crossing a long, low bridge over the harbour, just where it merged into the Cammerook River's tidal mouth, she sped past motionless fishermen, a waterfront restaurant, a children's playground. The houses petered out, and the highway shimmered with mirages in the midday summer heat.

Two minutes later, she had reached the turn-off to Moama. Bennett Parade was quiet, too. Sixty years ago, Moama had simply been the name of a beach. Thirty years ago, it had been a string of rustic holiday homes, most of them made of fibro-cement or weatherboard and set amongst dense and fragrant eucalyptus forest.

Now it was a town in its own right, prices for beachfront property had sky-rocketed and there were some gorgeous new houses looking out along the coastline of white beaches and rocky headlands. In another ten years, Arden and Moama would be seamlessly joined by the mushrooming developments.

The ambulance radio crackled into life, down near Hayley's left thigh.

'Informant is a four-year-old child, Car Seven,' said the dispatcher, Kathy Lowe. 'Repeating that, four years of age. She's sounding more and more distressed. Can I give her an update? Her name's Tori, by the way.'

'We're turning into Beach Road now,' Bruce said. 'Tell her to listen and she'll hear us coming. Tell her to open the front door.'

Hayley felt a prickle of apprehension. What was a four-year-old girl doing, reporting her own injury? Who was with her?

Kathy hadn't been able to get a lot of detail, although she was experienced and adept at talking callers through all sorts of emergencies. A former nurse, she'd recently coached a dad through the delivery of his wife's baby boy, over the phone, before the ambulance could reach the couple's isolated property. And she'd once pinpointed the location of two lost and lacerated tourists by correctly identifying the tree into which their car had slid on a muddy side road that they hadn't been able to name.

This time, Kathy had had to coax an address and other details out of a four-year-old. She was with her grandmother? Why wasn't Grandma helping to cook that boiled egg? Oh, Grandma was having a little nap? Was that it?

'She's crying too much,' Kathy had said. 'I can't get a good fix on what's wrong. Something about the grandmother. Something about the egg. Sounds like a burn or a scald.'

Hayley hated burns. Hated any injury to a child. Particularly hated it when no one had the presence of mind to plunge the burn immediately into cold running water, but how could you expect a four-year-old to think of that? Or to understand when Kathy had suggested it?

As for the grandmother...

'It's number 154—one of the new houses.' Bruce counted off. 'OK—146, 148. It's this one.' He pointed ahead to a dramatically beautiful architect-designed place, painted cream with purple-blue trim. 'Gee, look at the views it's got!'

The driveway climbed steeply upwards from the street, before finishing in a flat apron of paved stone in front of a double garage.

'I'm going to reverse in,' Hayley said, silencing the siren.

She passed the driveway, veered out wide into the street, then threw the gearstick into reverse and swung the steering-wheel hard down to the left, accelerating as she did so. The heavy vehicle lumbered backwards up the driveway, its engine loud and strident. Hayley craned in the driver's seat and managed the manoeuvre without difficulty.

Bruce was out of the car before it had even come to a stop. Hayley followed him through a sunny private courtyard newly planted with salt-tolerant shrubs and flowers and up the stone steps that led to a dramatic front balcony.

In the doorway stood Tori, a pretty child with a high ponytail of fair hair and brown eyes. Her pink cotton dress was wet all down the front and she was shivering and crying.

Shock? Hayley thought at once.

It was a possibility in a child of this age, if that water on her dress had started out scalding hot. The water must have hit...Hayley calculated quickly to give a very rough estimate...as much as eighteen per cent of Tori's total body area, possibly including a portion of the sensitive genital area. The symptoms she displayed could be the life-threatening medical condition known as shock, or it could be simply the aftermath of the body's adrenalin reaction.

Ahead of her, Bruce had picked the little girl up.

'I can feel the heat,' he said over his shoulder. 'Where's the kitchen? I'll get water on it before we ask questions.'

They went into the house, finding their way by instinct. Through a front hallway and a swing door straight ahead there was a large, ultra-modern kitchen and open-plan family room, overlooking a gorgeous rear deck and a gentle slope of garden, its lawn still just a tender new fuzz of green shading the carefully groomed earth.

Hayley overtook Bruce and found an American-style sink sprayer with an extendible hose and squeeze control. 'First piece of good news,' she said, pulling it out, turning it on and testing its temperature. It was fresh and cold, and the pressure was good.

'Look, the stove's still on,' Bruce observed. 'And here are two eggs cracked on the floor. And bread and butter fingers on a plate. You were trying to get some lunch, weren't you, Tori? Doing a pretty good job.'

A half-empty saucepan of water rested at a precarious angle at the edge of the stainless-steel stove top as well.

'Here we go, love.' Bruce sat Tori on the granite counter top and peeled off her dress, and Hayley began to irrigate the area of the burn. On the child's sandal-clad feet, she noticed two more patches of angry red and realised that there was further burning there as well. There were also some splashes on her thighs. Putting the plug in the sink, she let it partially fill to cover Tori's feet, then took the sandals off beneath the water, wishing she had two more hands.

'I know it hurts, sweetheart,' she said. Mentally, she added another three per cent to her estimate of the total burn area. 'This cool water will help, OK?'

'I'm going to see who else is around,' Bruce said. His voice dropped to an ominous growl. 'Someone had better be.'

He'd been in the ambulance service here for twenty years, with level four advanced life support qualifications, and he often claimed that nothing could surprise him any more. Plenty could anger him, though. Accidents to children that would have been prevented or made less severe by adequate adult supervision came close to the top of his list.

He handed Hayley a cotton blanket which she draped around Tori's narrow, shaking shoulders. The scalds needed to cool, but the rest of the child's body needed warmth. She needed the comfort of a friendly arm, too. Holding her, Hayley felt the spray from the sink hose dampen her white uniform shirt. She would be saturated before this was finished.

Tori's sobs had begun to subside into convulsive tremors. Her brown eyes were huge and tear-filled and she hadn't yet said a word.

'Is it not hurting so much now?' Hayley asked gently. 'Feeling a little bit better? We're here now, and we're going to look after you.'

She had a four-year-old herself. A boy named Max. Max's father lived in Melbourne now. Their divorce had been finalised for almost three years. Being on their own together, herself and Max, created a special closeness between mother and child, and Hayley was protective of the time Max spent with Chris. Chris loved his son, but that wasn't always enough.

Who loves this child? she wondered. Who is going to be devastated about this? Who is going to be guilt-ridden? Who is going to get blamed?

Above the sounds of Tori's sobs—she still hadn't spoken—Hayley heard Bruce's heavy footfalls on the tiles of the front hallway.

'Hello?' he called. 'Anyone here?'

He went to the back door and surveyed the unfinished garden, then headed left along the corridor to the bedrooms.

'We're going to take you in the ambulance in a minute,' Hayley said to the little girl. 'We're going to put some wet cloths on your tummy to keep it cool. Do you have a mummy or a daddy coming home soon?'

She was losing faith in the very existence of the grandmother, was beginning to believe that Kathy must have heard wrongly and that the child had been at home alone.

'I've got a daddy,' came a tiny voice at last, still shuddery and squeaky with sobs.

'Where's Daddy now, sweetheart?'

'At work.'

'Do you know where he works?'

'At the hospital.'

Bruce came back along the corridor, and entered another room just to the right of the hallway. Its door had been closed. Hayley heard his loud exclamation, and a few moments later his voice on the two-way radio, talking to the dispatch office. His words carried through the hall as far as the kitchen, easily clear enough for her to make out the words.

'Second car required at 154 Beach Road, Kathy. The grandmother wasn't taking a nap, Hayley,' he called, 'She's unconscious, and I'm going to check her out.'

'OK, I'm handling things here,' she yelled back to him.

It was axiomatic in the ambulance service—never leave the patient. That made things difficult in this case. They weren't a large station, and only one crew was on station duty during the day. A second on-call crew would have to be brought in, which slowed response time.

Meanwhile, Bruce would already be checking out the most obvious possibilities. An ECG would confirm or rule out a heart problem, while a quick test of the woman's blood-sugar level would indicate whether this was a diabetic coma.

After a few minutes, Bruce called to her again. 'It looks like a stroke.'

'You're sure?' Hayley asked. She continued to irrigate Tori's burned skin.

'The ECG isn't right for a heart problem. Her blood sugar's normal. But she's still unconscious, just lying here on the couch. That suggests CVA rather than TIA.'

'Yes, it does.'

She recognised the abbreviations. Cerebral vascular accident and transient ischaemic attack. The latter was sometimes called a mini-stroke, and rapid, complete recovery from this condition was much more common than from a CVA. The blocked blood vessel or leaking blood involved in the more serious event usually caused at least some permanent brain damage.

'I've checked her responses,' Bruce went on. 'She's reacting to pain and light. I've covered her and put her on her side, secured her airway. I'm going to keep talking to her, trying to get a response. How's your little heroine? Hayley, I don't want to leave until that second car gets here.'

'No, obviously not,' Hayley agreed, 'but it's difficult. She needs more than what I'm doing now, judging by her skin and her breathing.'

Tori looked clammy and pale, in contrast to her dark hair, and her breathing was too fast and too shallow. Her pulse was thready and rapid as well.

'Has she said anything?'

'She managed to tell me her daddy works at the hospital, didn't you, darling?'

'I wonder if he's there now,' Bruce said. 'We've no idea who he is?'

'No, but... Well, look at this fabulous house.'

'Yeah,' the older man agreed. 'There are more great views from this room. It limits the options. He's not the janitor. Doctor? Health Service Manager? I know him, and his kids aren't this age.'

Hayley was pulling sterile gauze pads from an equipment kit as they batted these questions around. Tori had paled further and was silent now, no longer in tears. Suddenly, her shoulders and stomach heaved, and she leaned forward and vomited.

Hayley took it in her stride, soothing the little girl, holding her shoulders more firmly as two more heaves came and rinsing the mess quickly down the sink when it was done. She gave Tori a glass of water, and the child spat out two or three mouthfuls then drank thirstily. Hayley turned off the sink sprayer and draped the soaked pieces of gauze over the area of the burn.

It was already beginning to blister, suggesting a partial thickness burn. Fortunately, the red area stopped a few centimetres below Tori's navel and her genital region had been spared.

'I'm going to get her settled in the ambulance,' she called to Bruce. 'When the others get here, we'll split crews, and Jim can drive me while Paul stays with you.'

She left the front door open and carried Tori to the ambulance, hoping the second car would get there soon. Tori looked tiny on the stretcher in the back of the car. Hayley covered her with a blanket at once. Next she inserted a drip, containing morphine for pain, and was alarmed rather than reassured by Tori's lack of fight when the sharp prick came. OK, yes, she'd found a nice vein in the back of the child's hand and the needle had gone in straight away, but she would have expected more of a protest.

She picked up the radio and spoke to the dispatcher. 'Kathy, is there a second car on its way?'

'Yes, Car Seven. Car Eleven just called in with a report on their status. It should be with you in a couple of minutes.'

'OK, thanks.' She turned back to Tori. 'What does Daddy do at the hospital, darling?' she asked. It would help if she could keep Tori alert and reassured.

'He's Dr Black,' came a weak little voice. 'He makes people better.'

'Dr Black?' Hayley echoed. She went cold.

Dear God, it had to be Byron! This was Byron Black's daughter…

In the distance, the siren of the second car could faintly be heard. Meanwhile, Hayley's mind raced. She'd seen him, what, twice, in sixteen years? They'd trained together in Arden's competitive amateur swimming club in their teens. Most people had called him B.J. then, but they probably didn't any more. She hadn't used the nickname herself, even back then. She hadn't felt that it suited him.

He was three years older than she was, but they'd both been backstroke specialists, tackling the sprint distances. This had meant a lot of cheering for each other, a lot of powering alongside each other in the pool and the growth of a friendship. They'd both been keen and competitive, thriving on the atmosphere, and they'd made it to the state championships twice.

Once, they'd even kissed. Lord, she hadn't relived that delicious memory in years...

Then, when Hayley had been fifteen, Byron had gone off to Sydney to study medicine at Sydney University, and it had seemed as if he'd made a permanent life for himself in the city. He'd been openly competitive in the pool, and he was obviously ambitious about his career. He didn't come from a professional background. His father worked in a local hardware store, and Byron had had to work hard towards each new goal. In hindsight, she had the impression that he gloried in a challenge, and she couldn't think of any goal he'd set and failed to meet.

Hayley had run into him once on the beach around Christmas-time about seven years previously, in the company of a pretty, dark-haired woman. 'This is my wife, Elizabeth,' he'd said. She had introduced him to Chris that day, and the four of them had talked for a short while.

A couple of years later, they'd bumped into each other in the supermarket and had exchanged two minutes of superficial news. She'd heard a couple of things since. That Elizabeth had died in a plane accident of some kind. That they'd had a little girl.

Tori.

The sirens grew louder and the lower tone of the

vehicle's engine joined the noise as it grew closer. Then the sounds of sirens and engine both died. The second ambulance was here, parked in the street below.

Climbing out the back of her car, Hayley directed Paul Cotter up to the house. 'Bruce is in the living room with the other patient. First door on the right,' she told Jim Sheldon. 'You're driving this car. Let's go.'

'Righto, Hayley.' Paul hurried up the steps, his black trouser legs a blur, to disappear inside and find Bruce.

Hayley climbed back into the car to Tori.

'We're going now,' she said, gently peeling back the blanket and replacing the gauze, warmed from Tori's over-heated skin, with freshly soaked pieces. 'We're going to see Daddy at the hospital.'

'Daddy…' said a tiny voice.

A few weeks ago, Hayley had found out that Byron was coming back to Arden with his little daughter to oversee the accident and emergency department at Arden Hospital and act as Resident Medical Officer. He must have started work there already, judging by what Tori had said. He was replacing an older man who'd retired. But Hayley hadn't seen him yet because she'd been in Melbourne for the past two weeks, giving Max some time with his dad.

Her heart did a familiar, uncomfortable flip. Chris had been his usual difficult self during her visit. He'd hinted at the possibility that the two of them might get back together. His wistfulness on the issue was a vindication of the way she'd suffered when he'd left, but beyond that... It didn't seem to have occurred to him that perhaps she'd moved on.

'You're my best friend, Hayley,' he had whispered to her. 'Maybe that's what really counts.'

Her reply had been stiff. 'I'll always be your friend, Chris.'

He'd been her first and only lover. He'd been her husband for seven years, and he was the father of her child. Aware of all his faults, she still cared for him. It wasn't a particularly rewarding feeling but, with Max's needs to consider, was she just being selfish to want more?

She had driven the eight hours back to Arden in a state of unsettled questioning and hadn't given a further thought to that trivial yet oddly pleasant piece of news, a few weeks earlier, about Byron Black's imminent return.

And now, here she was, on her second shift back, sitting in the back of Car Seven with Byron's injured daughter. Dear God, he would be racked over this.

The driver's door of the car slammed shut and Jim started the engine. 'How is she?' he asked.

'Pretty shocked.'

'And the other patient?'

'Bruce didn't have chance to give me much of a report. He's pretty sure it's a stroke. They'll just have to see how it resolves once she's admitted. She must be in her sixties.' She would have liked to have said more, to tell Jim, She must be either Byron Black's mother or his mother-in-law. How's he going to feel?

But Tori needed her attention. It wasn't the time for gossip and conjecture with Jim.

'We're on our way now, sweetheart,' she said, taking the child's soft little hand. 'It won't be long. I'm going to get Mr Sheldon to talk to the hospital and tell your daddy that you're coming.'

But Tori didn't speak. She had her eyes closed now. Hayley left her hand where it was.

'Jim, I've worked out who she is,' Hayley told him briefly and quietly, twisting towards the front of the vehicle. 'Can you contact the hospital and make sure Dr Black is available in A and E?'

Jim whistled. 'His daughter? The new guy? I handed over to him last week, another CVA. He seemed good—thorough, focused, not too arrogant—but he's going to be a mess today.'

He was.

Hayley glimpsed him standing in the ambulance bay as they pulled in. He hadn't changed much since the last time she'd seen him. He still had the broad shoulders of a swimmer, still wore his thick, soft hair short so that it would stand up in dark spikes when he towelled it dry…or when he ran his fingers through it in agitation, as he was doing now.

He had brown eyes. They weren't puppy brown like Chris's, however, but tiger brown with a glint of gold, an altogether more dangerous colour. He had a long straight nose, a wide, serious mouth and a broad forehead. Each of those features was stiff with tension now. They appeared to be etched more strongly than usual, as if the sculptor who'd made him—and any sculptor would be proud to have made a human form like Byron Black's—had dug his tools in extra deep, manipulating them with force.

There had always been an aura around Byron, something that hinted at the capacity for deep-running passion and the capacity to contain that passion carefully inside him. Today it looked as if the passion was threatening to break free.

A nurse and an orderly appeared with a stretcher and a drip stand. Hayley opened the back of the car, unlocked the ambulance stretcher from its metal track and slid it out, extending the wheels down to ground level as she did so. Tori was light and little and easy to shift from one stretcher to the other.

'Tori! Victoria!' Byron said hoarsely, curving his long body over her.

He was in the way of the drip line, but Hayley managed to snake it around him. As she did so, the sensitive inner skin of her forearm brushed across the top of that dark, spiky head and his hair was as silky and clean as she remembered. With the hairs of her arm still standing on end, she passed the plastic bag of fluid across to the nurse, who hung it on her stand.

An orderly began to wheel the stretcher inside. Byron was still leaning over it, his long, strong legs working instinctively to keep up as they rumbled from concrete slab to vinyl flooring, through a set of automatic doors.

'Daddy...' came a little voice, fuzzy from the effect of the morphine. 'Grandma wouldn't wake up from her sleep.'

He went white, straightened like a released catapult and turned to Hayley, blind and helpless. Didn't even recognise her. She wasn't surprised. 'What happened?' he said. 'What on earth happened?'

'She has a partial thickness burn over twelve to fifteen per cent of her body.' Hayley kept her voice calm and impersonal. He needed a clear report, not a lot of words wasted in sympathy. Not yet. 'No facial or genital involvement. The other patient in the house with her appears to have had a CVA and she's coming in a second vehicle. The other crew will be able to give you a better report on her status…'

'A CVA? That's my mother…' Byron was paler than ever now. 'Dear God, and the two of them were alone!'

They could all hear the sirens of the second ambulance now. Byron clearly didn't know which way to turn next, his usual control and authority momentarily deserting him. His eyes looked wild, his lips were white, his fists were balled hard. Hayley ached with sympathy for him.

'Tori must have been terrified,' he whispered.

'I think she wasn't, Byron, not until she burned herself,' she reassured him, using his first name without even thinking about it. 'She was trying to make boiled eggs for lunch. She thought your mother was just having a little sleep on the couch.'

'All right, yes. I guess that's how she would interpret it, yes.' His vision cleared suddenly, emphasising the golden glints in the depths of his eyes. 'Hayley! Hayley Kennett! I'm sorry, I've only just…' He gripped her arm.

'It's OK.'

She returned his gesture, squeezing the muscular forearm she'd seen so many times, tanned and dripping wet, at swim practice. With an arm like that, it felt as if he should be the strong one but, of course, he wasn't today, not after what had happened. She didn't waste time reminding him that she was Hayley

Morris now. She hadn't gone back to her maiden name after the divorce.

'We don't know how long she spent trying to rouse her grandmother,' she said instead, as they covered the final few metres before entering the paediatric section of the emergency department. 'Perhaps no time at all. She does seem to have taken the "nap" at face value. Her dress was wet all down the front, and there are burns on her thighs and feet, suggesting that she tipped boiling water over herself when she was trying to get the eggs out of the saucepan. We found the eggs broken on the floor.'

'Mum's all right?'

He stood back for a moment as they transferred Tori from ambulance stretcher to emergency department bed. Its fresh starched white linens were stretched smoothly across a firm mattress, and it was surrounded by equipment and supplies whose intimidating effect could only be partially offset by pictures of dinosaurs, landscapes and fairies on the walls.

'She's in the care of our second crew.' Hayley repeated herself patiently. 'Bruce McDonald is with her. He ruled out a heart problem and diabetes, secured her airway and was trying to stimulate her into waking up when I left. I can't say any more than that yet.'

'This is a nightmare!' Byron muttered helplessly.

Then he turned to the A and E nurse, and was suddenly in complete control. Only on the surface, Hayley suspected. Only because he had to be.

'Get whoever's on call to come in *now*,' he said. 'We need a second doctor. Tori, Daddy's here, sweetheart. OK, we need her on monitors. Hayley, how fast are you running that drip? You have her on morphine, right? How much? Tori, you're fine, now. You were scared, weren't you, and you were brave and just brilliant to phone the emergency number like that, and remember our new address. I'm so proud of you. Daddy's going to have a look at your tummy and your feet now, OK?'

Hayley answered his questions, darting her responses into his uninterrupted flow of words. After recognising her, he hadn't looked at her again. He had pulled a chair up beside Tori's bed and hadn't looked away from his daughter since he'd released that brief, almost painful squeeze on Hayley's arm.

She stepped back with a reluctance that surprised her. Her role in this was over, apart from writing up her reports, but she didn't feel ready to let go. She wanted to look after Byron, which was strange when they'd had so little contact over the years. He was so big and capable, so determined, strong-willed and confident. It was unsettling, heart-rending, to see him this vulnerable.

She wanted to make promises and assurances to him that she had no right to make. Things like, It wasn't your fault. They're both going to be all right. Don't knock yourself out.

But she was just a casual friend from years ago, someone he'd yelled encouragement to and slapped on the back in congratulation. Someone he'd kissed just once, in the corner on a couch in the dark at a party.

It had lasted for, oh, at least an hour—a first, wonderful taste of the primal intimacy that a man and a woman could find together. Then a couple of days later he'd turned up at her front door to say something awkward about his imminent move to Sydney and not wanting to get involved in a relationship at the moment.

To tell the truth, she'd been relieved to hear it. At fifteen, just a girl, not a woman, she hadn't been ready for a serious relationship with a university-aged boyfriend who already seemed to know exactly what he wanted out of life. For a few months she'd had romantic dreams about meeting up with him again when she was a mature adult—say, seventeen or eighteen—but then those dreams had drifted into insignificance, as a young girl's dreams so often did, and at nineteen she'd met Chris.

The automatic doors opened again as Bruce and Paul wheeled Mrs Black into A and E. A second nurse came forward to take formal charge of the new patient. As Hayley sat at the desk at the A and E nurses' station, she heard Bruce giving a more detailed rundown on Mrs Black's condition.

'Blood pressure one-sixty over ninety. Pulse eighty-seven. Oxygen saturation ninety-eight per cent.'

When she was leaving, she heard Byron's voice again. 'Where do we have beds at the moment? High Dependency?' Then a few seconds later, decisively, 'No, I'm not sending her to Sydney. We can treat her here. I'm not letting her out of my sight.'

Jim had moved Car Seven away from the ambulance entrance. Hayley took the passenger seat and they drove away at the leisurely pace which came as a relief after the urgency of earlier.

'Want to call Dispatch and tell Kathy we'll take that patient transport now?' Jim suggested.

'Yes, we're much later than scheduled,' she agreed, then spoke into the radio. 'Dispatch, this is Car Seven...'

The numbers of the cars implied a large ambulance fleet, but since the lower numbers belonged to vehicles now retired from service this was deceptive. This rural area didn't need a large fleet. There was one crew on station duty day and night, seven days a week, with a second crew as back-up on call. Very often, the back-up crew wouldn't be needed for an entire shift.

Hayley and Bruce had been diverted from the non-urgent patient transport job earlier when the urgent call-out had come.

The patient transport in this case was nearly a two-hour job, door to door. They went to a dairy farm about thirty kilometres from town where an elderly man was ready for the local hospice, in the terminal stage of his illness. After delivering him there and handing him over to the hospice staff, they returned to Ambulance Headquarters at three o'clock, and the rest of the day went by with no call-outs. Jim and Paul had gone home, while Bruce joined Hayley to finish their shift at the station.

'Wonder how that little girl and her grandmother are getting on,' Bruce said after they'd signed out for the day. He added before Hayley could answer, 'Going straight home?'

She had showered and changed into black stretch jeans and a soft blue knit cotton top. 'No,' she answered. 'I'm going to phone and find out how Max and Mum are getting on. If everything's all right, I'm going back to the hospital.'

CHAPTER TWO

THE sight of his daughter in sleep was something that Byron had treated himself to every single day since her birth four and a half years ago. There was so much trust displayed in the way a happy child slept. The skin around her eyes and across her forehead was completely innocent of tension, and she slept on her back as if always prepared for the brush of his goodnight kiss.

Watching Tori sleep was like a compass point in his life, he sometimes thought. It kept him on course. After Elizabeth's tragic death, when Tori had been just six months old, the sight had become even more necessary, and even more precious. Sometimes it was the only time in a whole day when there was stillness and quiet.

The time when he wasn't run off his feet at work, juggling six things at once, always the one people looked to for answers and solutions. When he wasn't trying to remember the items on the shopping list he'd left at home, or fighting hospital administration over budgets and legal issues. He wasn't swamped by onslaughts of Tori's irrepressible exuberance and curiosity.

He didn't have to say, Sit down at the table, Tori, we don't stand up on a chair when we eat, or Don't jump on the couch, love. You'll break it and you could fall and hit your head on the coffee table, or

Time to put your toys away now. Yes, it is, it's almost bedtime!

Every night when he came into her room before going to bed himself, just to look at the little form tucked under the covers, breathing so deeply and rhythmically and peacefully, he felt a fullness in his chest that was pure love.

He hadn't thought there could be a stronger or deeper feeling for one's child. Today, watching her in her white hospital bed in the high-dependency unit, with the summer light still bright and hot in the non-air-conditioned room at the end of the day, he discovered that he'd been wrong. There was a stronger feeling, and it came when love was mixed with fear. It weakened his limbs and made him light-headed and he hated it.

He'd almost lost her today. It reminded him too strongly of the way he'd lost Elizabeth four years ago in a tragic accident which for months had tortured and taunted him with pointless, impotent if onlys. He didn't think that way about Elizabeth's death any more.

Or not often, anyway. He'd accepted it.

She had received an invitation from her GP practice partner and his wife to fly with them in their light plane to Tamworth for a weekend of country music, line dancing and outdoor meals. Byron himself had insisted—maybe he'd been too high-handed about it—that she needed a break. She should go and he'd be fine with Tori, who had been a pretty exhausting child even then.

'I'll only go if I've expressed enough milk, and if

we've practised with her taking a bottle from you,'
Elizabeth had said.

*Don't think about what would have happened if
Tori had refused to take a bottle.*

Tori had taken to the bottle with no trouble at all,
and so Elizabeth had gone to Tamworth. There had
been a mechanical failure. The plane had crashed into
the wild country of the Dividing Range, near
Barrington Tops. All five people on the aircraft had
been killed instantly, but it had taken State
Emergency Service volunteers and other rescue work-
ers more than four days to locate the wreckage. When
they finally had, it at least had provided a form of
certainty and reality to the tragedy.

It had happened.

Now there had been another accident, and there
was a new set of if onlys.

If only Elizabeth's parents hadn't decided to move
north to Queensland to be closer to their other two
children. Byron still felt uneasy about their move.

He wondered if Elizabeth's mother had been unhappy about looking after Tori full time while he was
working. If so, she should have said. Had that been
the problem? It had seemed so sudden, and their reasons had been vague at best.

He had thought this many times over the past few
months, hated this sort of powerless questioning at
the best of times. He vastly preferred a situation
where he could take action, and where he knew exactly what he was dealing with.

And was he wrong to have returned to Arden? It
had seemed like the right thing to do. The obvious
thing to do. An action he *could* take. He'd made his

home and his career in Sydney mainly because that had been where Elizabeth had wanted to be. Theirs had been the kind of partnership where both of them had made willing sacrifices.

But then his widowed mother had been keen to see more of him and Tori, and had insisted that she'd be fine looking after her granddaughter while Byron was at work.

'After all, she'll be in preschool for three mornings a week this year,' his mother had said. 'I'll get a break. And it's not as if she's still a Terrible Two.'

No, but she was a pretty full-on four and a half!

He should have insisted that it was too much for Mum. She'd looked so tired when he'd come home each day, but she'd kept saying that everything was fine, that she loved it, that Tori was no trouble. Since when had Tori ever been 'no trouble'?

Even Elizabeth's mother Monica, who was active and energetic and only fifty-four, would throw up her hands some days and say, 'Take her home! I've had enough!'

Mum was sixty-eight.

In the bed, his daughter stirred and moaned, and Byron's eyes pricked with stinging tears that he steeled himself not to give way to.

Victoria Louise Galloway Black had a personality even bigger than her name. She was so bright, so confident. Dangerously so, it had proved. She wouldn't have thought twice about getting lunch on her own for herself and Grandma. Her favourite, of course, soft-boiled eggs with bread-and-butter fingers to dip into the runny orange yolk.

And he kept wondering about the 'nap', too. He

knew that Mum and Tori watched children's TV shows together on the ABC in the late afternoons. *Play School* and *Madeline* and *Bob The Builder*. Maybe today wasn't the first time Mum had taken a nap on the couch. She often fell asleep in front of the television at night, he knew.

Did Tori regularly end up pottering around by herself, having ideas more ambitious than her small hands could manage, while Mum snoozed?

He should have insisted that it was too much…

Byron heard a soft movement behind him and turned, expecting it to be Tori's nurse, come to carry out her scheduled set of observations. Instead, it was Hayley Kennett. Except, no, she wasn't Kennett any more, he remembered vaguely. She'd married Chris someone. Only…wasn't she divorced now? Someone had passed on that bit of news to him. So perhaps it was Kennett again, after all.

He ransacked his brain, trying to fill in the landscape of her life in more detail, but couldn't do it. He also felt bad that he hadn't recognised her at first today. She had always been one of the nicest girls at swim club—fun-loving, hard-working, competitive and zestful, with a body as sleek as a seal's and no falseness in the way she'd congratulated those who'd been more successful than her.

He wasn't surprised that she'd succeeded in the demanding career she had chosen. The New South Wales Ambulance Service often received over a thousand applications for every advertised trainee position. Odds like that wouldn't have scared Hayley off.

'Hello,' she said quietly. 'I wanted to see how she was getting on. And your mother.'

'I'm sorry I didn't recognise you today.' He touched her hand briefly. It was pleasantly cool.

She shook her head, and her dangling earrings caught the light. 'You had other things to think about.'

'Thank you for being there.'

'I was just doing my job.'

'You're not doing it now, though. You didn't need to follow up.'

'I wanted to.'

'I really appreciate it, Hayley.'

It was the sort of thing that you said anyway, but he discovered, as he tasted the words in his mouth, that he really meant them. What was this new feeling that had been nagging at him lately? Whatever it was, the sight of Hayley made it diminish immediately. Something uncoiled inside him, and the perpetual tightness at his temples and in the back of his throat slowly and fractionally eased.

'How's Tori?' she asked.

They both looked down at the sleeping child. Byron knew that she was the most beautiful child in the whole world, with her creamy skin and long lashes and fine, blond-streaked light brown hair. He accepted that there was perhaps a tiny hint of parental bias in his opinion, and that other people didn't think the same way, but that was their problem!

'We pulled her through the real danger—the shock—and she's stable now,' he said. 'Kidney output is good. We're still giving her a lot of fluid, high pain relief. There's very little full-thickness burning. She'll only need a couple of small grafts, which I can take her to Canberra for. Thank heavens. I keep thinking, if she hadn't known how to dial OOO... If she hadn't remembered our address...'

'But she did. Those what ifs are dangerous, Byron,' Hayley said. 'What if she hadn't burned herself at all, and she'd gone on thinking that your mother was just having a sleep? Your mum could have lost her airway while she was unconscious and choked to death. Maybe Tori's burns have saved your mother's life.'

'Don't follow it any further.' He shook his head, his closed mouth firm and tight, then added, 'You're right. I'm thinking too much, when action is what I prefer. I checked on Mum a few minutes ago, across the corridor, and she's asleep as well. Otherwise I'd take you across, so she could thank you. I mean,' he revised, 'she's not talking yet, but she was squeezing my hand earlier.'

'That's good.'

'She's looking a lot better than she did at first. Look, have you eaten? Would you like to grab something? What is it?' He looked at his watch. 'Just after six? We could...catch up, or something.'

Dear Lord, what was that odd little thread in his voice? he wondered. Was it shaking?

'Uh, well, I was about to head home,' Hayley answered him reluctantly.

She saw the disappointment in his face at once, and guessed its source. He was restless, anguished. He didn't want to eat with just the company of his own tortured thoughts tonight.

'But I could hold off on that,' she added quickly. 'Just for an hour or so. My son's with my mother.'

'I'm sorry,' he answered. 'No, please, keep to your plans.'

'Look, I'll phone her, OK? Max is probably fine to stay a bit longer. He's very comfortable at Mum's, and she was going to feed us anyway. I'm not rostered tomorrow, and I'm taking him to his first preschool session. He and I get to see plenty of each other.'

'Tori's starting preschool, too. Supposed to be,' he revised in a bleak tone. 'Is your son going to Arden North?'

'Yes, it's just around the corner from us.'

'And it's halfway between my place and the hospital. I live at— Well, you know where I live.'

'It's a beautiful house,' she offered. 'So dramatic and cleverly designed. You must have enjoyed getting it right, and once you've got the garden going…'

Byron shook his head. 'It's not beautiful to me at the moment. Stupid to blame the house for what happened!'

'Pizza?' she suggested, to change the subject. He looked as if he wanted to veer away from it—like a racing driver taking a tight turn.

'Sounds good.' It was automatic, and Hayley guessed that he didn't care what they ate.

'I'll ring Mum and Max from my mobile when we get outside,' she said. 'Want to take my car?'

'Whatever…'

She suspected he might have more male ego at stake on the issue normally, but tonight he either didn't care or he realised, as she did, that he was too preoccupied to be safe at the wheel. The latter, probably. She somehow had the impression he'd become a man who kept pretty close tabs on his own emotions.

'Something's come up,' she said to her mother on

the phone. 'Could you handle it if I'm not there till about seven-thirty or so?'

'We're fine. Not a problem, I hope?'

'I'll tell you later.'

It was almost comical to watch Byron folding himself into her small car. Chris always refused to drive with her at all. 'That thing? I'd rather walk! Come on, look at me! Do you think I'd fit? We'll take my car.'

Byron was tactful enough not to comment on the dimensions of the car. Perhaps he didn't care tonight. He had his knees tipped sideways and pressed hard against the door, and a painfully tight frown on his face.

Hayley didn't try to talk to him as they drove. He probably wanted to make this quick, and he might well end up regretting that he'd asked her. She'd seen enough of the way people behaved in a crisis to know that moods could swing back and forth like the boom of a runaway yacht in a storm.

There were two pizza restaurants in Arden, and she picked the closest, able to park directly in front of it because it was early and a week-night.

'Whatever you like' was his preference in toppings.

Helpful! But she didn't want to push, didn't want to waste time and energy over something that trivial. Suddenly remembered the pizza nights they'd had after swim meets and confidently told the man behind the counter, 'Large ham and pineapple, please.'

'Take-away?'

'No, to eat here, thanks.' There! Easily dealt with!

There were four tables at the back. Plastic tablecloths. Postcard-style prints of Sicily on the cheaply panelled walls. Red vinyl tiles on the floor. The place wasn't glamorous.

And it could have been the bottom of a stairwell full of garbage cans for all Byron cared, Hayley realised.

She was swept with a churning wave of tenderness for him. Perhaps it was the kind of thing you could only feel for the man who used to be the boy who'd given you your first real kiss. They'd never had a falling-out. Life had just swept them off in different directions. Heaps of the girls at swim club had had crushes on him, but he'd been too focused on his goals to even know it, and too honorable to have taken advantage of those silly female hormones if he had.

And now he'd grown up. He was a man in every sense of the word. Thirty-four years old, successful in his profession, with a physique that had more than adequately filled its adolescent promise. He had known a man's joys, and the unique grief of losing a spouse, which didn't touch most people until they were well into old age.

Without thinking about how he might interpret the gesture, she stretched her arm across the table and covered the back of his hand with her palm and fingers, chafing his warm, smooth skin gently.

'She must be an amazing little girl, Byron,' she said. 'I'm looking forward to meeting her properly at preschool. Maybe Max will have met his match at last.'

'I'll believe that when I see it!'

He laughed and gave his hand a half-turn so that his fingers met Hayley's and actively returned her touch. He squeezed her fingers, then stroked the ball of his thumb back and forth over her knuckles. It was slow and hypnotic. Shouldn't have been erotic as well, but it was, and suddenly Hayley remembered in exact and vivid detail just how good that kiss of theirs had been, sixteen years ago.

Slow, questing, exploratory. Not a prelude to a more intimate goal, but the goal itself. Just to kiss. Just to hold each other. Just to melt inside. She had mussed up his hair. Those short, dark strands weren't spiky at all, but soft and slippery and clean.

He had slipped his hand beneath the hem of her top and the waistband of her jeans to touch her skin. It must have taken him half an hour to reach her breast. He'd caressed the neat, firm swell the way he was caressing her fingers now, slowly and without demands.

'It's good to see you again, Hayley,' he said at last. It sounded as if he meant it, but it was clearly an effort all the same.

'Mmm, it was a good time in our lives, wasn't it?' she answered. 'Those years in swim club? We had fun.'

'Do you still see any of the others? Any people from that group of us who went to state championships two years in a row?'

'Craig's still around. Samantha. Rob.' She sketched a summary of their lives, and mentioned one or two others as well who'd left Arden and moved to bigger places like Sydney or Melbourne or Canberra.

'And what about you?' he asked. 'You and—?'

'Chris and I are divorced,' she came in quickly.

For some reason, it was important to get this across very clearly. Important for whom? Byron? Or herself?

'I'd heard, I think.' He nodded.

Their pizza arrived, giving Hayley the excuse—she suddenly needed it—to pull her hand away. She felt disloyal to Chris, touching another man's hand and enjoying the sensation so much. It was crazy. Chris had been the one to leave. He had wanted to 'find himself'. He hadn't been able to 'handle being a father'. She'd 'sprung it on him'.

His problem. All of it.

She had seen some signs, on her recent trip to Melbourne, that Chris was growing up at last. Maybe he had 'found himself' now. He'd started a self-defence school the previous year, called the Cee-Jay International Tae Kwon Do Academy, and was working hard to recruit students. If he kept it up, the school would provide him with a decent income. He still couldn't manage his accounts or his taxes, but she didn't mind helping him out with those from time to time. She didn't want to see him fail. Which meant she still cared. Enough to—?

'Yes, it's tough,' Byron said.

She jumped at his words, and realised she'd been miles away, hardly tasting the salt of the ham and melted cheese and the juicy sweetness of the pineapple. 'I'm sorry,' she said.

'I get the impression that the break-up wasn't your idea,' he clarified.

'Uh, no. No, it wasn't. I'm...stubborn. I don't like to let things go, or admit defeat before I've given it everything I've got. And I have Max's needs to consider.'

He nodded and didn't pursue it, which she was relieved about. Why had she told him all that?

'I'm not brilliant company tonight, am I?' he said instead.

'I wasn't expecting you to be.'

'Thanks for that.' He pressed his palms against his eyes and let out a gust of breath. 'When something like this happens— I mean, I miss Elizabeth badly enough at the best of times, but when something like this happens…'

'I know.' She nodded.

Although she didn't, of course. Not truly. A divorce wasn't the same thing as a death. The pain was focused in different places.

'I've stopped looking for it to go away,' he said. 'I used to try and measure it. I'd think, It's less today than it was a month ago. I'm healing. But I've stopped doing that. Because it's not linear, is it?'

'No.' That she could agree with, in full understanding. 'Not at all.'

'It goes up and down like—like share prices on a stock-exchange index or something.'

'Bad today,' she guessed, and out came her hand again, reaching across to his.

'Pretty bad,' he confirmed, and returned her touch for the second time. 'Four years! Some people have married again after four years.'

He shook his head.

'Do you think you'll ever remarry?' It should have been an intrusive question, but somehow it wasn't.

Byron shook his head again. 'No, I don't expect so. Just can't imagine that I could ever find that…that *totality* again. Bits of it, maybe. The physical part. Or the friendship. But not the whole of it, not the certainty of it, not in one person. Not the same.'

'No, it wouldn't be the same,' she agreed, out of that same tenderness she'd felt for him before.

'I've had it, though. I've been lucky. A lot of people don't even get it once.'

'No…'

Their hands separated and they each ate a little more pizza in silence.

Hayley thought, He's romanticising. But who wouldn't, after what he's lost? He obviously did love her very much, and now that she's gone, he's forgotten the tensions they must have had, the disagreements, the disillusionments. Everybody has them!

It was one of the things that made her wonder—uncomfortably—if she and Chris could still have a future together. She understood him, she cared about him, he was Max's father. What more did she want?

'I've been away from her long enough,' Byron was saying, and for a second Hayley thought he was still talking about Elizabeth. 'I don't want her to wake up when I'm not there.'

Oh, he meant Tori, of course!

'Nor Mum, for that matter,' he said. 'I'm hoping my aunt and uncle will come down from Harpoon Bay to see her tomorrow.' He pushed back his chair. 'Unfortunately my younger sister lives in London now.'

'You haven't finished your pizza.'

He waved it away. 'Take it home with you, if you want.'

She asked for a box, and when they got back to the hospital she hunted up one of the nurses in the high-dependency unit and said, 'Can you...kind of...*remind* Dr Black to finish this off during the night?' She didn't have to ask to know that he wasn't planning to go home before morning. 'Heat it up in the microwave for him even? Put it on a plate and shove it into his hands?'

'Not looking after himself properly?' the nurse guessed.

Hayley cannoned into the man himself in the doorway to this section of the unit. He'd checked that Tori was still asleep, and was about to cross the corridor to see his mother.

'Still here?' he said.

'Your pizza's in the fridge,' she answered drily, earning his rusty laugh.

'I thought it was your pizza,' he said.

'No, it's definitely yours. I'm not all that fond of ham and pineapple.' She added, before he could ask, 'That was what we always used to get when we all went out after swim meets, remember? Mr Hazelwood didn't used to give us a choice, or he said we'd have been there all night, making up our minds. I saw his point!'

'And you never said you didn't like it?'

'I wasn't going to be the only nuisance.'

'You were always too nice!'

'So were you. You used to wait before you took the last piece.'

'Not very noble of me, since I knew Mum would have a second dinner waiting at home.'

'You mean she didn't know about the pizza?'

'Hey, I was growing!'

They both laughed.

With one hand propped against the doorway, he leaned down and cupped his other palm against the back of her neck, his fingers nestling into the feathery texture of her short, dark hair. Instinctively, she lifted her face and their eyes met, and she saw an awareness in his gaze that she knew was mirrored in her own.

His pupils were wide and dark, and there was a new softness to the way he held himself. Now he was watching her mouth. Her lips parted on a sudden in-breath, her heartbeat quickened and then he released his hold and the moment passed.

It was a relief. She wasn't prepared for something like this tonight.

'I m-must get to Mum and Dad's to pick up Max,' she stammered. 'Don't lose touch now that you're back.'

Big points for inanity on that one, Hayley!

'I won't,' Byron said. He might have said more, but she was already striding off along the corridor.

He watched her for a moment.

It was visiting hour, and there were knots of people about, some of them looking distinctly uncomfortable in the hospital environment. Hayley took no notice of them, kept her head down and her walk rapid so that her delicate gold and jade earrings swung against her slender neck and caught the light. He'd noticed that before.

Speed seemed to suit Hayley, Byron decided. She had been fast in the pool, she was fast at the wheel of an ambulance and she was fast on her feet. Organised. Efficient.

Escaping.

He knew it. Was deeply glad she felt the same way

he did about that little moment of heat in the doorway, and about the way their hands had kept straying together across the restaurant table as they'd talked. He'd always found her very attractive. She was compact yet strong, with gorgeously smooth skin and a constant sparkle of life and warmth in her dark brown eyes.

Of course they'd all been a mass of stimulated hormones at swim club, surrounded by all that slick, wet skin and smoothly honed muscle. He had fancied almost all the girls at one stage or another, even the ones he hadn't particularly liked.

Perhaps that was how he'd learned so early on that you had to divorce physical attraction from emotional connection. When he'd met Elizabeth during his second year of medicine at Sydney University, their physical response to each other had been just one part of the package—the uniquely precious and complete package he knew he'd never find again. Didn't even want to find again, in fact.

These days, he didn't have that scatter-gun, adolescent approach to women. Only during those late teen years had he fancied anything and everything in a skirt. The sit-up-and-howl feeling came much less often, now. There was discrimination involved.

And yet he still found Hayley Kennett...or whatever her surname was now...very attractive indeed. Found that their long-ago kiss was surprisingly vivid in his memory. It unsettled him. Scared him, if he was honest.

No. Definitely. I don't need it. I don't want it.

It was an instinctive thing, and not something he

wanted to analyse too closely. Wasn't the reluctance enough? Did he have to work out *why*?

Yes. Perhaps he did. Take a deep breath and just do it, Byron.

He didn't fully trust his judgement, or his reactions—that was part of the problem. It would be so easy to numb himself...assuage certain needs...with an affair, kidding himself that it was safe with Hayley because they'd known each other for so long. But what would happen when the affair ended and the numbness wore off? He'd be back to square one, and minus an old friend. Worse, he'd have lanced open the still-not-fully-healed wound of Elizabeth's loss and the agony would be back.

No, if he was going to launch into any kind of new relationship, now that he was back in Arden, it wouldn't be with Hayley, he decided firmly. It would be with someone much, much safer.

On that note, feeling relieved, he went in to see his mother.

CHAPTER THREE

'MUMMY'S on roster today,' Max told his preschool teacher, Karen, on a Wednesday morning in late March. 'That means she's staying all morning.'

'I know. It'll be fun having Mummy, won't it?' Karen agreed, smiling across the top of the little boy's mid-brown head at Hayley.

'What do you need me to do, Karen?' Hayley asked. She hadn't been the parent on roster at pre-school before, although she'd done it several times the previous year when Max had attended a junior play school for two short mornings each week.

But before the teacher could answer, they were both distracted by the sight of Byron Black stepping up to the veranda, with his little girl's hand in his. He was so tall that he almost had to duck to clear the low veranda ceiling, and there was something about him that had already drawn more than one pair of eyes.

'Excuse me, Hayley,' Karen said. 'This is little Tori Black, and it's her first day. She's…uh…had a rather difficult time.'

'That's fine. I know Tori. And her dad,' Hayley said.

She couldn't help watching the pair as they came through the door. In the bright morning light, Byron looked anxious at first, as if wondering whether Tori was ready for this yet. His reaction made sense. It was six weeks since the little girl's accident, and her burns didn't show, but beneath her pretty purple sundress there would still be significant scarring, as well as areas of reddened skin like latticework where she'd recently had her grafts.

Karen went forward to greet them, while Hayley dropped to the carpet to help Max with his jigsaw puzzle of a cat. She was well aware that her thoughts were focused on Byron and Tori more than on the wooden pieces scattered over the carpet in front of her.

'I did this one every day last week,' Max said. 'I know it off by heart.' Which explained why he didn't actually need her help at all. 'Ear. Tail. Other ear. Head. Paws,' he said, his fingers snapping each piece unerringly into place.

Being superfluous to Max's puzzle-doing, Hayley felt less guilty about her continued awareness of Byron and his daughter. She had gone to the hospital to visit Tori and Mrs Black one more time, two days after the accident, and had given Tori a three-dimensional puzzle set, but Byron hadn't been there at the time. The handovers she'd made in the A and E department since then had been made to other members of staff.

She'd heard some news of him, though, via another ambulance officer who had also known him during their high school years.

'He's started going out with Wendy Piper, who's my wife's GP,' Paul Cotter had said. 'Good luck to them, and I hope he likes horses!'

'Dr Piper's my GP too,' Hayley had replied cautiously. In Arden's compact health-care system, this meant that Dr Piper also worked at the hospital in certain capacities, including regular rosters in the A and E department. 'But I hadn't heard about her and Dr Black.'

'Oh, she and my wife are friends as well. Rhonda's keeping a horse for Wendy at the moment, too, so they meet up in a muddy paddock sometimes. Have a good gossip, I expect.'

Karen showed Tori where to hang her small pink backpack, where to put her piece of fruit and where the toilets were. Byron hovered just behind them, alert for any potential problem. Leading the little girl over to the puzzle shelf, the preschool teacher then said encouragingly, 'Why don't you choose one and your dad can help you with it?'

'I'm good at puzzles. I love puzzles. I don't need help, but he can *join in*,' Tori corrected firmly.

'Would you like to join in, Dad?' Karen said, with a smile in her voice.

'Love to!'

There! He'd also smiled now at last and it was amazing how much it changed his face. The warmth was something you could have heated your hands by. There was a generosity in it, too. Share my pleasure, it seemed to say. Love and loss weren't the only emotions that touched this man through and through. Hayley found that she was smiling as well, although he hadn't even looked at her yet.

Byron managed to find a space on the carpet that was big enough to accommodate his long legs and sat down, while Tori chose a puzzle. He caught sight of Hayley and they both said hello. Max noticed, and informed Byron, 'Mummy's on roster.'

'Will she need some help?'

'I don't think so.'

'Are you staying?' Hayley guessed.

He shifted a little closer, and spoke quietly. 'Yes, it's probably not necessary, but her graft sites are still tender, and— Well, I just wanted to stay for her first day, that's all.'

'You can cut up the children's fruit,' Hayley suggested, 'and then it won't feel as if you're just hovering.'

'That's a good idea.' He looked relieved. 'It'll be good to be involved, at least this once. Mostly she's going to be brought here and picked up by her home day-care mother.'

'Is that working out well?'

'Wonderfully well. She's been going to Robyn's for two weeks, and I've heard only glowing reports from both of them. I even,' he confessed, 'dropped in unannounced last week. You know, you hear stories about bad child-care...'

'I know.' Hayley nodded.

'But Robyn had Tori and the other two she looks after, plus her own little boy, out in the sandpit, making roads and gardens out of twigs. All their sunhats were on, and she was making them a healthy snack. I felt like a heel for checking up on her in such an obvious way.'

'Hadn't you thought of an excuse for your visit?' she teased.

'No.' He grinned wryly. 'I'd squeezed it in between working out next month's A and E doctors' on-call roster and following up on a problem we've been having with some equipment. I had to take time off work because of Tori's burns, and things have been hectic since I started back, so I just wasn't thinking. Kicked myself for not at least handing over a spare pair of socks or something.'

'Since the day-care mother is a parent herself, she'll understand.'

'She *did* understand! Instantly! Might have been less embarrassing if she hadn't! Doting father, caught red-handed in an act of flagrant worrying.'

Hayley laughed. Despite that fleeting look of anxiety as he'd entered the preschool, he seemed a hundred times more relaxed than he had been six weeks ago. More confident, too—confident enough to mock his own feelings. The softer, happier expression suited his face, and the confidence suited his voice. It was lazy, deep and rich, lacking the harshness of fear and agitation she'd noticed that day in February.

'How is your mother?' she asked.

His face fell a little. 'She's still in rehab, but progressing well. Taking a few steps with a frame. Saying a few words. Feeding herself, left-handed. It's going to be a long road, and we haven't made any plans yet, but she's motivated and that's a huge plus.'

'It is,' Hayley agreed.

'Your mother looks after Max, you said?' His interest seemed genuine, and she remembered that from the past as well. He probably wouldn't have described himself as a good listener, but he genuinely was.

'Yes, and Dad pitches in, too,' she explained, 'with bedtime stories when I'm on a late shift, and trips to the playground. I couldn't manage a paramedic's hours without them.'

Chris's parents lived locally, too, but unfortunately

they weren't very interested. Even during her marriage, Hayley had never been very close to them.

'They're in good health, obviously,' Byron said, still talking about Hayley's own parents.

'Very, thank goodness,' she answered. 'Dad'll be sixty next year, but you wouldn't know it.'

'My in-laws are like that,' he said. 'Monica's coming for a visit next week. Tori can't wait, and I'm looking forward to it, too. She's a terrific woman.'

There wasn't much time to talk after this. The children packed away their puzzles and had group time and news. With a preschooler's short attention span, these things didn't last long. Then it was time for 'activities'—all the craft and play tasks that were so important in building a child's fine motor skills. Karen asked Byron if he could help one child at a time on the computer as they learned to manipulate the mouse and played a shape-matching game.

Hayley was fully occupied in writing names on paintings and pegging them out to dry, as well as helping Karen and her assistant in encouraging the children's ideas and reminding them to take turns and share. She was still aware of him in the room, however, his deeper voice a low counterpoint to the high-pitched tones of children.

More aware than she wanted to be, if she was honest. He'd already betrayed the fact that any attraction on his part was reluctant. Not wanted. With Chris still talking on the phone about 'getting back to what we had', Hayley didn't—*shouldn't*—want this awareness either.

Next came a session of singing and drama, and

Byron asked Hayley, 'Where's this fruit I'm supposed to cut up?'

'There, on the sink in a bowl. Ask Karen about how to do it, because some things get peeled and some don't, and there are particular ways she likes it cut.'

'Who knew fruit was this complicated?' she heard him mutter to himself at the sink a few minutes later, as she was wiping down the craft tables. She had to smile.

Yet he didn't look nearly as out of place as many fathers she'd seen in a setting that was mainly the province of women and young children, despite his height and imposing build.

Chris, for example, didn't always find the right tone. He tended to use a high-pitched, overly sweet voice, and say, 'Wow! That's incredible!' a lot, when he didn't really mean it.

'It's just a block tower, Daddy,' she'd heard Max say to him once. 'I can make much better ones than that.'

'Talk to him like a person, Chris, for heaven's sake!' Hayley had lashed out at him one day.

'OK, I know. I'm not used to it, that's the trouble. Every time I see him, he's grown. I never said I'd be good at this, did I? You sprang it on me. That's why the whole thing fell apart. We weren't planning on having kids for another five years.'

'It takes two, Chris.'

'Are you saying you weren't the one who got careless?' he'd answered, his voice rising.

That's right, she remembered now. Her criticism had led to one of their worst arguments and, though she'd fought hard for her own point of view, she had to concede he had been right about some things. Unconsciously, she had got careless, hadn't she? She'd foolishly thought that a baby wouldn't be a problem for them.

Complicated. Love, parenthood, divorce. All of it was complicated.

At the end of the preschool session, Hayley saw an attractively dressed woman with red-brown curls waiting outside the gate, and realised that it was Dr Piper.

'How's the play-dough?' Wendy Piper said to Byron.

'Sticky.'

'Yuck!' It was cheerful, but there was an edge.

Tori looked up at Dr Piper gravely, holding her father's hand. She didn't say hello until prompted by her father. Hayley slipped past them with Max, who said a cheerful, 'Bye, Tori.'

'Bye, boy!' she answered, and added in a stage whisper to Byron, 'I haven't learned his name yet. I'll learn all their names adventurely.'

Oh, 'eventually'! In Tori's innocently self-important tone, it had been a cute mistake.

'I'm going to show you my horses today, Victoria,' Dr Piper said, with bright yet distant friendliness. 'After we've been to a nice seafood restaurant for lunch. Do you like prawns?'

'No, they have feelers and eyes.'

Hayley suppressed a giggle. Perhaps she ought not to be enjoying the miscommunications between doctor and four-year-old, but she was!

'Let's go home, Max,' she said, ushering him to her car and getting out her keys.

She wasn't due at Ambulance Headquarters for her shift until just before six that night. Her service worked a standard 'four on, four off' roster—two day shifts, followed by two night shifts, and then four days' break. It was workable, as a single parent, but only with her own parents' tireless support.

'Bye, Hayley,' Byron called out after her, as she strapped Max into his seat belt. Dr Piper echoed his words with a brief, uncertain smile in Hayley's direction. Possibly Dr Piper hadn't recognised her out of context.

'Thanks for the wisdom about the fruit,' Byron added. 'Apparently I still did the banana wrong, but I think Karen's forgiven me.'

'What was that about?' Wendy asked him in a possessive yet lightly amused tone.

But Hayley didn't hear his answer, because she'd closed the car door.

The strident ring of the hotline at Ambulance Headquarters broke into what had been a quiet shift. Hayley had been watching television and getting sleepy at almost eleven o'clock. She hadn't been able to decide whether to head off to an uncertain night's sleep in one of the stand-down rooms, or to curl up in the reclining chair where she currently sat.

The hotline suggested she wouldn't have to make the choice.

Bruce got there first, and reported succinctly when he'd put down the phone, 'Accident on the highway near the state border.' Their station covered the isolated area that straddled the border between Victoria and their own state of New South Wales. 'It sounds serious. One car, two injured.'

Hayley fought off sleep and lethargic muscles, pulled up the overalls she'd peeled down to her waist and was ready to go. Bruce took the wheel, and she was happy with that. It was an isolated, winding stretch of highway. Not an easy drive in the dark.

'What else do we know?' she asked as they pulled out of the driveway, sirens already whooping.

'A passer-by phoned it in on his mobile, but he had to drive a fair way beyond the crash scene to get within signal range. He's going back to the scene now, so he can flag us down. Says the car's hard to spot from this direction. He didn't actually witness the crash and isn't sure how long ago it happened.'

'So it might have been several minutes before he even got there.'

'Longer, on that stretch of road, on a weeknight.'

'Did he check them out?'

'He has no first-aid or emergency training so he was reluctant to do anything.'

'Which was the right thinking. How near the border?'

'Don't know. Dispatch didn't have any more details. They've got the second crew on standby. We've got road rescue and police on the way, too.'

'So it could be forty kilometres?'

'Fifty, if "near the border" means on the Victorian side.'

'I *hate* that stretch of highway!'

Hayley shivered. She'd driven it many times over

the past couple of years, taking Max to visit his father in Melbourne.

Once out of town, on the Princes Highway, heading south, Bruce brought the car's speed up to the edge of safety. It was a Thursday night, just over a week after Tori Black's first day at preschool, and the road was deserted. The shadows of the eucalyptus trees reared strangely in the powerful headlights, and the road's many bends made it anything but a relaxing drive.

At one point, they saw a wombat lumbering along at the grassy edge of the highway's shoulder, and Bruce clicked his tongue. 'This isn't the place for you, little mate,' he said.

On a straight stretch, they glimpsed the blue lights of a police car behind them, with a fire brigade vehicle close on its tail.

'We'll get there first, unless that lot push their pedal down harder,' Bruce commented.

The journey took twenty minutes, and they must have been just a few kilometres shy of the state border between Victoria and New South Wales, marked by a couple of nondescript signs, when they came upon the scene.

The man who had phoned in the emergency call stood on the verge of the road with a torch in his hand, waving the beam around to attract their attention. He was pacing in agitation, and he ran up to Hayley's window as soon as Bruce had stopped the vehicle.

'There!' he said, directing his torch beam into the thick eucalyptus forest. 'See it? Against that tree, right off the road. One of them is moaning. The other hasn't moved. I—I didn't have a clue what to do.'

Bruce wheeled the ambulance around and backed it up to the crippled car. It was an older model, with dents and patched, rusty paintwork. The whole of one front corner was crumpled like a sheet of unwanted paper. There were two men in the vehicle—in their early twenties, Hayley guessed.

One of them, his legs trapped by jagged folds of metal, was ominously limp and still, and Bruce's quick examination confirmed that he was dead. 'No hurry, I'm afraid. Which is…good—if you can use that word—because it would have been a job to cut him out fast.' His voice was thick with frustration.

The other man, the driver, was still moaning thinly, and the way his body was angled in the seat wasn't right. At least he wasn't as badly trapped. His pulse was thready, though—more than 140 beats per minute—and his systolic blood pressure was barely half what it should have been.

'Internal bleeding,' Hayley told Bruce, who nodded. 'We'll use the anti-shock suit once we've got him out. His airway's good.'

'I can smell petrol,' Bruce answered quietly. 'I'm glad these blokes are here.'

He thumbed over his shoulder. The fire crew was assessing the scene for likelihood of fire or an explosion, while another team was preparing to cut away the crumpled front of the car.

'Would have happened by now, wouldn't it?' Hayley said in an undertone. 'Anyway, we can't think about it…'

She had a clear face mask over the injured man,

delivering oxygen at fourteen litres a minute, while Bruce was positioning a neck brace in case of a fracture.

'It's OK, mate,' he said in a clear, cheerful tone to their patient. 'We're going to get you to hospital in a minute. We're looking after you now.'

Had the man understood? The moans were unchanged in sound.

Next, Hayley searched for a vein into which she could insert a drip, but the man's rock-bottom blood pressure had deflated his blood vessels like punctured balloons.

'Can they get us some better light? I just can't see enough in here.' As she spoke, one of the fire people rigged up a lamp and she moved a little to get the near-lifeless arm into the light. 'Track marks here already, Bruce,' she observed softly. 'Gee, that's going to make it easier!'

'Not!' her partner answered.

But she did find a vein at last through which to pump the blood substitute which they hoped would keep him going until they reached the hospital. She also set up a heart monitor and took a blood sample, and one of the rescue vehicles set off with it at once for Arden so the process of cross-matching for a transfusion could commence sooner.

'OK, I think we can bring him out,' Bruce reported to the fire crew a few minutes later.

'Pulse has dropped a bit, and blood pressure's climbing,' Hayley said. 'That's great. Yes, let's move him now.'

With difficulty, they slid him from the mangled car on a spinal board and transferred him to the back of the ambulance. Just this movement was enough to negate any improvement in his condition, and the heart monitor showed a weak, galloping beat. The SouthCare helicopter was already on its way, as there was no doubt he'd need the care provided at a major hospital.

The MAST suit was their last resort, and the time had come to use it. Medical Anti-Shock Trousers had been a military invention adapted for medical use after the Second World War. Fitting from the feet to the abdomen, they could be inflated to artificially pressurise a patient's legs.

This had several benefits. Most importantly, it pushed blood away from the extremities towards the brain and other vital organs. It could also act to lessen internal bleeding, and effectively splinted a patient's injured legs. Once the patient reached hospital, it was then critically important to keep the suit inflated and in position until blood replacement had begun.

The suit worked as desired, and Hayley could report to Bruce, 'OK, he's as stable as we can make him. Pulse and pressure improving again. Let's go.'

'On our way.' Bruce activated lights and sirens, and acknowledged the police and fire teams who were still busy at the scene.

'Feel that?' Hayley told the unconscious patient as the ambulance sped up. 'We're on our way. We're going to get you to hospital. Hang in there, OK? You're fine.'

But he wasn't. The improvement in his heart rate and blood pressure had flattened now, well before reaching the level she'd been hoping for. He'd stopped moaning, and his unconscious state seemed to be deepening. He wasn't fine, and in her heart she knew it.

Dear Lord, he reminded her so much of Chris—blond, casually dressed, good-looking in a rough sort of way—and Chris always took this road too fast! Hayley could never resist asking him, 'What time did you leave Melbourne?' And the answer always added up to an impatient, unbroken journey, usually overnight.

She was always left then with images of just such a scene as she'd witnessed tonight—a lonely car, crumpled against a huge tree, because Chris had fallen asleep at the wheel, lost control on a bend, been blinded by a rare set of oncoming headlights, or braked too hard, avoiding a wombat or a kangaroo.

The danger was so real she could almost reach out and touch it. There was even an advertising campaign on television about the road toll in Australian country areas, a heart-rending litany of examples, recited by the family members and friends left behind.

But whenever she asked him—*begged* him sometimes—to slow down, take coffee-breaks, drive by day and stop for a decent lunch, he always denied that it was a problem.

'I know my limits, Hayley. I never drink. I drive to the conditions. You should see me if it's wet or foggy! I crawl. You only worry because of your job.'

'Yes, and I wish you had my job sometimes so you'd take it a little more seriously!'

'Don't be so self-righteous!'

Another one of their arguments, their standard lines to each other as familiar as a well-rehearsed play. She'd been thinking a lot about those arguments lately, it seemed. Self-righteous? She didn't think of herself as a self-righteous person.

Not that she had time to think about it now. She did what more she could in the ambulance. It wasn't much, and that pulse rate was rising again, while the man's systolic blood pressure was back down below seventy. The tracing on the ECG finally went flat five minutes south of Arden, and Hayley spent the rest of the journey frantically trying to resuscitate him.

Intubation first, so that she could provide artificial ventilation. CPR, which she couldn't combine with any other treatment while she was on her own. She just didn't have enough pairs of hands. They reached the hospital, where Byron and Wendy were both already waiting in Emergency as Bruce pulled into the ambulance bay.

Wendy had her curly hair wound into a knot on top of her head, and was dressed, like Byron, in green surgical scrubs. They were prepared for surgery, or to assist with further stabilising and transferring the patient between ambulance and helicopter. Byron looked rumpled and in need of his morning shave. They both had their shoulders hunched as if they were cold.

Hayley continued CPR, while Byron and Wendy started drug therapy in an attempt to get the patient's heart working again. Hayley began her handover report as they moved the man inside, and at a bigger hospital she would have ceded full responsibility to the medical staff as soon as she'd finished what she needed to say. Here, with fewer hospital staff on hand, she continued her involvement.

Byron administered atropine and adrenalin, as well

as the universal blood type, O-negative, but after a further ten minutes of frantic work Hayley knew it was no use. Byron pronounced death and resuscitation attempts ceased.

Wendy swore and closed her eyes.

'Sorry to get both of you out of bed in a hurry for a result like this,' Bruce said to the two doctors gruffly.

It was up to hospital staff to handle the rest of the formalities from now on. The SouthCare helicopter was notified, and headed back to base.

Back at the station, there were no more call-outs and Hayley managed to get a fitful night's sleep before she went off shift in time to pick up Max from home—her mother had stayed with him overnight—to take him to preschool. It was one of those times when she couldn't shake off the pall of the night's work, and it seemed incongruous to be here at this sunny, innocent play place.

Incongruous, but like balm to the soul. They had arrived several minutes early, and the sliding glass doors of the preschool were still closed as Karen and her assistant prepared for the day's session. Max wanted to play on the outdoor equipment while they waited, so Hayley watched him.

With his repeated cries of 'Watch me, Mummy!' it would have been difficult to do anything else.

Soon she was laughing. 'You are just *flying* off the end of that slippery-dip, Max!'

'I like going fast. Can you push me on the swing now, please, Mummy?'

So she did that, too, standing in front of him and giving his knees a gentle shove. She pretended to tickle him each time he got close enough, and they both laughed some more. Then suddenly Max let out a shriek of delight.

'Daddy!' He jumped off the swing too fast and promptly fell over, but scrambled to his feet again at once and ran towards the preschool gate.

Hayley turned in astonishment to see Chris standing there, fit and blonder than ever in a sleeveless shirt that showed off his summer tan and his strong muscles.

He's bleached his hair, Hayley thought. It suits him...

'Daddy!' Max exclaimed again, and flung himself into his father's arms as soon as Chris had fumbled open the child-proof catch on the gate.

'Hi, little mate!' he said, his voice high. He pretended to wrestle Max to the ground like a wild animal. 'Hi, Hayl,' he added cheerfully.

'Chris, what on earth are you doing here?'

'You told me on the phone how much fun it was, coming to preschool with Max, so I thought I'd give it a go.'

'But you have classes tonight, don't you? It's term time. Didn't you have classes last night?'

He shrugged. 'It's fine. I'll make it back for the adult classes this evening. I've got one of the brown belts taking the kids for me today.' His eyes looked creased and bleary.

'You drove all night.' She felt sick. 'You can't drive straight back. You're talking about two eight-hour journeys, back to back, with a busy morning and no sleep in between.'

'Oh, preschool is that tiring?' he teased. 'Anyway,

I grabbed an hour's sleep at Mum and Dad's, as well as a good hot breakfast.'

'Two people got killed on that road last night.' Her voice was low, but the passionate anger in it was unmistakable. After what she'd dealt with last night, him turning up today of all days wasn't well timed. Several parents and children were arriving now, and Karen had opened the sliding door, but Hayley didn't care.

'Yeah, I saw the car, I think,' Chris answered her with a careless sort of curiosity. 'There was still a heap of glass on the road. It looked pretty bad.'

'It *was* bad, Chris! Dear Lord, does it need to be *said* that two people getting killed is bad? You know how I feel about this!'

Her voice was shaking and it had risen in pitch now. Out of the corner of her eye, over by the second preschool gate, she saw Byron and Tori arriving with an older woman whom she didn't recognise. She felt...*ugly* somehow at being caught out by Byron like this, yelling at her ex-husband in a state of high emotion.

Chris gave a disgusted sound as if Hayley was the whole problem, and pivoted on the balls of his feet to face Max, who wasn't paying any attention to the exchange between his divorced parents.

Is he so used to it? Hayley wondered, mortified. Is that it? Or...or...maybe we're subtle enough about it that he doesn't realise, and he's just bored. I hope it's that...

She clung to the idea, knowing she was kidding herself. Max's cheerful face was screwed up tightly now.

'Hey, tiger, are you going to take me inside and do a painting for me?' Chris asked his son, overly bright in tone.

He grabbed Max's hand, and headed inside. Hayley had knots at her temples now. Why did they always do this to each other?

Suddenly, she realised that Byron was watching her, deliberately rather than casually, and that he'd seen the strain and anger in her face. He let the woman—probably Elizabeth's mother, Hayley decided—take Tori inside and stepped off the veranda towards her.

'You look quite shaken up. Are you still thinking about last night?' he said when he reached her, leaning down a little because he was so much taller. He touched her arm, a trailing caress that her stiffly held body didn't encourage. His fingers soon dropped, and perversely she wanted them back.

'It's…uh…not one of my favourite parts of the job. I'm sorry,' she answered him.

'Lord, you don't have to apologise! If it's any consolation—'

'I can tell you now, it won't be!' she cut in on a laugh.

'No, I suppose not.' He sighed. 'But I'll tell you anyhow.'

'Yes, please, do,' she answered, feeling very clumsy and still burning inside after her argument with Chris. She didn't usually interrupt people like that.

'Well, they weren't the most mournable people in the world, it turns out. Wanted by the police in

Melbourne, and carrying a saleable quantity of hard drugs in the car. No family they were close to.'

'Oh, so if Max's father crashes his car on that road I'll feel OK because, after all, we were already divorced so I shouldn't care any more?'

He paled and tensed at her uncontrolled tone. 'No. My God! No.'

'I'm sorry. I'm sorry, Byron.' She felt her scalp tighten all over. 'That was…pretty bad.' Looking at his startled face, she realised that she had to explain. 'Chris just turned up straight from Melbourne, that's all, and he's planning to drive back as soon as the preschool session is finished. He goes fast and he never takes a break. I—It's been a sore point between us for a while.'

'Yes, I can see that,' he drawled. It wasn't unsympathetic.

'It's—I don't think it's safe, and we've just had another fight about it. He…' she laughed jerkily '…can't get it into his head that I'm angry at him because he's Max's father and I actually *care*, not because I'm a prim, disapproving little spoilsport. But I had no right to inflict any of that on you. No right at all!'

'Hayley…' Byron stopped, still looking very stiff.

She jumped in. 'Look, it's not your problem and I apologise again for pulling you into the crossfire.'

'It's all right, and I understand. That's when it's hard, isn't it? When our work resonates with something that's happening at home. I remember a couple of years ago when some casualties were brought in after a light plane crash-landed at Bankstown Airport.

It was—' Once again, he stopped abruptly, then added, 'Took me weeks.'

She didn't need to ask, Weeks to what? Just nodded instead. Felt his hand squeeze hers briefly as well. It was large, firm, strong, just like the rest of him. This time her stance didn't repel the gesture, and the warmth of their contact lingered for several seconds before his hand came away, trailing a last touch across the sensitive pads of her fingers as it went.

Still standing close, she caught the faint scent of him, shower-fresh and woodsy, and had a melting urge to pillow her forehead on his shoulder, as if seeking an infusion of his male strength. Self-reliance, competence and control got *old* sometimes. What would it be like to lean against a man like this and say, Look after me. Not all the time. I'll do my share. But just for today...

She didn't do it, or say it of course. Instead, she took a deep breath and a small backward step, confused by what she felt.

'Could you hide his keys or something?' Byron suggested.

'Like good friends do for a mate who's been drinking?' She shook her head. 'I don't think so.'

'The only practical suggestion I could think of.'

'And I appreciate it. Practical suggestions can be thin on the ground. But he'd—No, it wouldn't help with the underlying stuff. We'd only get angry at each other again.'

'And he'd drive faster to prove a point,' he said gently. 'And you'd worry more.'

'I expect so. Let's go inside,' she suggested

quickly, wanting to put the whole conversation behind her.

There was something very tempting about Byron's apparent understanding and, instead of awkwardness, she was left with a glimpse of something tantalising, like a beautiful, sun-filled garden seen through a half-open door.

'Yes, let's go in,' he was saying, 'because I'd like to introduce you to Elizabeth's mother.'

At first impression, Monica Galloway reminded Hayley of her own mother in many ways. 'I enjoy a multi-generational friendship network,' Adele Kennett often said, with a twinkle in her eye which apologised for the elaborate phrasing. Elizabeth Black's mother put it more simply, during several minutes of conversation she had with Hayley.

'I love being around littlies,' she said. 'I'm going to have a lovely morning with this swarm. Your Max looks as if he keeps you on your toes.'

'Oh, yes! But he's getting more settled as he gets older.'

'Byron mentioned how thankful he was to have you on the scene the day Tori burned herself.'

'Did he?' Hayley was aware of a warm glow rising into her cheeks, but then she heard Chris's voice and it distracted her.

'Mate, we've done it twice. Let's pick another puzzle.'

'But I want to do the fire engine again.'

'No, mate…'

Let him do the fire engine again, Hayley begged her ex-husband silently, frowning in his direction. He's not being rude about it, and it's no big deal. He likes to do all the puzzles over and over. *Let him, Chris.*

She was embarrassed to find that Monica had followed her gaze. It was obviously a morning for awkwardness and apologies.

'He...uh...doesn't see quite enough of Max to know when to...'

She trailed off, feeling as if every conversational step she took ended in a puddle of emotional quicksand. Did Mrs Galloway really care about any of that? She was tactful enough not to comment.

'Byron's frowning at me,' she said. 'We're supposed to be having coffee with a friend of his this morning.'

'Oh, that'll be nice,' Hayley agreed politely.

Hayley dragged herself reluctantly away from preschool a few minutes later, still feeling tired and tense.

Perhaps I should have taken Byron's advice and found a way to 'lose' Chris's keys, she thought. Because I'm going to spend the rest of the day angry and worried and waiting until I can phone tonight to check that he's safely arrived home.

CHAPTER FOUR

'OH, BUT my horses *are* my children, Monica, and so are my cats,' Wendy said cheerfully.

She smiled across at Byron, inviting him to share her mild amusement at Monica's tunnel vision on certain issues. He did, tokenly, but felt no desire to leap to either woman's support in what would soon, he foresaw, become a genteel battle of diametrically opposed forces.

His sense of distance was like a familiar garment, worn so many times since Elizabeth's death that sometimes it felt like a permanent part of him. He knew it was unnatural. He wasn't normally the type who sat back and observed, but he didn't know how to get his old self back again.

'It's not the same, though, is it?' his mother-in-law answered.

'Isn't it?' Wendy said, her eyes still twinkling, but at Monica herself this time. 'Horses and children both take an inordinate amount of time and money, can be extremely temperamental and come with absolutely zero guarantee of providing a desirable outcome. *I* think it's identical! Except that I can sell a particular horse if it's not working out for me and I'd probably get in trouble if I tried to sell a child.'

'It's *not* the same,' Monica repeated, just as cheerful but stubborn on top of it. 'You'll realise that the moment you have one.''

'Well, yes, except that I probably won't,' Wendy said. The deference and apology in her tone was token. 'Have any, I mean. It's honestly not high on my agenda. I have a very full and satisfying life without the presence of small people in it, and I don't think it would be very honest of me to bow to social pressure and manufacture a dubious maternal instinct at this late stage!'

'And, of course, you're absolutely right to look at it that way, if that's the way you feel,' Monica agreed energetically. 'It's refreshing to find a woman who really knows her own mind. Wonderful! So can I please hear more about your horses and cats?'

Oh, dear, she really doesn't like Wendy, Byron thought, retiring mentally to an even greater distance from the conversation.

When Monica started gushing and agreeing to that extent about something Byron knew she didn't, in fact, agree about at all, it meant she had crossed the person off her list completely. If she liked Wendy, she would be getting wistful by now and trying to persuade her that she really would actually like just one tiny weeny little baby, really she would.

Oh, crikey, I suppose I'll have to think about this...

Byron poked at his feelings for a bit, with an enormous sense of fatigue and distaste for the process, while Wendy told some well-crafted anecdotes about her horses.

Monica didn't like Wendy, and there was something very unnatural about the way they were talking. That should bother him a lot. He should be feeling uncomfortable and disappointed, because he respected Monica's judgement, and yet...

He finally discovered that what he really felt consisted mainly of relief.

I'll stop seeing her. I'm obviously not ready. And Monica obviously agrees I'm not ready, and that's why she's washed her hands of Wendy. And if Wendy mattered, then it would bother me. But she doesn't matter. Which is why I went out with her in the first place. So obviously that's not the answer to what's eating at me. I'll have to tell her—Wendy—as soon as possible that it's been a mistake and I don't think there's been any harm done.

He had no reason to think that she was seriously smitten.

Byron discovered that he felt the way he always felt when he'd emerged unscathed from the dentist. He was giddy, light-hearted and the whole world seemed like a better place.

For heaven's sake, why have I been going out with her if it's been that much of a burden? he wondered.

He thought about it a little more, with less reluctance this time, and came up with two reasons. Firstly and most importantly, there had been his acute reaction to Tori's burns, seven weeks ago. He was convinced that she needed more competent, loving adults in her life. She needed a new mother, which meant, logically—throat tight, temples throbbing—that Byron needed a new wife. Only one way to go about that. Start at the beginning.

But Tori's burns were healing fast. His terror and remorse had ebbed now, and she was as confident and sunny as she'd always been. Robyn was working out so well as a day-care mother that his feelings had subsided to a manageable level, and Robyn's younger sister Simone was more than happy to stay at his place overnight when he had to work.

And, oh, dear Lord, he didn't want to get married again! He'd known love. The love of his life. He was grateful for that. But it was gone.

Unfortunately, however, he was...lonely. It had separated itself out now as a different feeling from simply aching for Elizabeth. He still felt her loss like a large, heavy stone in the bottom of his stomach, but the stone was slowly shrinking to a more bearable size, and beyond this loss he had begun to distinguish a more generalised yearning. He had a name for it now.

Loneliness.

He was lonely for the light, musical sound of a woman's voice in his home, and for the comfortable, attractive touches a woman added to a man's domestic world, even as a casual visitor. He yearned for someone with whom to indulge in rambling conversations, walks on the beach and take-away dinners in front of video movies while Tori slept.

His body had awakened physically, too. He'd begun to understand that, yes, he would now find it very possible to go to bed with a woman who wasn't Elizabeth. He noticed women in the street, and not with the gut-twisting thought, Her walk—or her hair, or her figure—is just like Elizabeth's, but with a little kick of urgent, unthinking, visceral male desire.

Perhaps all of these points added up to why he had picked Wendy. She gave off the impression—he wasn't sure if it was intentional—that she wouldn't need to feel completely committed to a relationship

in order to sleep with someone, and that would suit
both his wariness and his increasingly impatient need.

But apparently there was still too large a part of
him that wasn't ready after all, because they hadn't
reached the point of sleeping together and relief was
still singing its siren song in his ears, far more
strongly than his desire for Wendy had ever sung, and
he hadn't heard a word that either woman had said
for the past five minutes.

Just as he thought this, Monica laughed aloud.

Glancing across and catching his eye, Wendy apologised, 'Byron's heard this story before.'

'Well, it's a good one,' Monica said. 'But I think
we're keeping Byron against his will. You need to get
some things done this morning, don't you, B.J.?'

What? Byron thought. No, I don't! You're obviously ready to leave yourself.

'B.J.?' Wendy echoed, meanwhile.

'Don't start,' he warned her. 'There's a list of
who's allowed to call me that, and I'm not adding
more names to it.'

Wendy pretended affront, and drawled, 'Oh, I see!'

'I think he'd take my name off that list if he could,'
Monica said, 'only I'm too much in the habit of it
now. He's right, of course. It isn't appropriate for a
man in his position.'

Monica's a kind person, Byron thought, his distance falling back into place. Wendy hadn't got a clue
that she hadn't made the right impression.

'Yes, I do need to run a few errands,' he an-
nounced, and saw a tiny flare of...gratitude in
Monica's face.

'Yes, and I should get out to a certain muddy paddock to coddle those terrible four-footed children of mine,' Wendy agreed.

Casually, she took care of the bill and had said goodbye and left before Monica had finished fumbling for something in her bag.

'OK, you're right,' Byron told his mother-in-law somewhat grimly. 'And don't pretend that you don't know what I mean.'

'No, well, she's a perfectly nice person, but...'

'I'm going to drop you home while I run those fictional errands,' he threatened lightly, 'And you'll be bored there, and it'll serve you right.'

He went to the local department store and bought a dress for Tori, a quirky vase and some potted plants for the house, for no good reason except that he was still thinking about the way women brightened their homes. His new place still needed...something. Something more than just a growing garden and some new pieces of furniture.

Then, at twelve-thirty, he went through the pre-school gate to pick up his daughter.

As he was leaving with her a few minutes later, he overheard Hayley saying to her ex-husband, 'The blond streaks suit you, Chris.' She looked terrific herself, in cropped navy pants, a matching top and dangling gold earrings. Her dark hair glinted with rich red-gold lights as it moved in the mild breeze, and her brown eyes sparkled with life as always.

Chris's reply was indirect and, from the tone, a spur-of-the-moment impulse. 'Hayley, do you know what? I'm going to ring Melbourne and cancel tonight's classes. I'll offer a free make-up class at the end of term. Then I can stay over and drive back first thing in the morning. Are you working tonight?'

'Yes.' She gave a wide yawn. 'I got a few hours' sleep this morning, though, as well as some overnight at the station, so I'm fine. And I have four days off, starting tomorrow.'

'So we can go to the beach together with Max this afternoon, and I'll sleep at your place before I head out tomorrow. Give your parents a night off.'

'That'd be great, Chris. Oh, I'd *really* appreciate that!'

The relief and warmth in her voice were palpable, and Byron felt an odd twist of something that resembled envy, just below his heart. Hayley's loneliness and her needs weren't remotely the same as his. It seemed very probable that she and Chris still had a chance.

'Come on, Tori,' he said, just a bit too cheerfully. 'I'm going to take you home to Nana, and then I need to go to work.'

He saw Hayley again that night, or rather in the early hours of the following morning. He'd rostered himself for several night shifts while Monica was visiting, feeling that he still had a debt to repay in that area after the way the local doctors with visiting rights at the hospital had stepped in to cover his absence during Tori's recovery.

They'd had a slow but steady stream of patients through A and E since he'd come in to work just after lunch, but now things were quiet. There was one young pregnant woman just getting ready to go home. She had begun a slow bleed and had come in for reassurance he wasn't fully able to give.

The cervix wasn't dilated, she'd had no cramping and the trickle of blood looked old, lacking the frank red of a fresh flow. But when he'd felt her uterus it wasn't quite as big as he'd have liked it to be for the date she'd given. He confirmed that this was the start of a slow miscarriage, but that there was nothing to be done about it now.

He had an asthmatic child and her mother as well, who had been there for two hours while he'd got the eight-year-old's breathing under control. She would be on her way up to the children's ward in a minute because he still wasn't happy with her blood gases and he sensed that both mother and child felt safer where help was close at hand.

Now, just as his energy levels reached the nadir that came around four in the morning, he heard the siren of an incoming ambulance. Here were Hayley and Paul Cotter, one of the men who'd brought his mother in here seven weeks ago, unloading an older male patient from the back of their vehicle with the calm efficiency and reassuring stream of conversation which experienced ambulance officers usually displayed.

It was much easier than last night. Like Hayley, he found it hard to shake off any loss of life on the roads, but this was something different, and much more common.

'Chest pain,' she reported. 'And I think this one's for real.'

Quite a high percentage of them weren't. Indigestion, a pulled muscle and even flu could all present with the patient or a loved one making a panicky diagnosis of heart attack.

This man, though…

Hayley gave a quick rundown of the man's name, age, weight and other details, as she and Paul ran the wheeled ambulance stretcher up the short ramp that led to the emergency entrance. 'He looks like a classic,' she reported. 'Writhing in pain, described it as ten out of ten, radiating into the left arm.'

'Here we go, Stan, almost there,' Paul told the patient.

'OK, let's get you settled in and take a good look at you, Mr Frewin,' Byron said. He noted the man's ashen colour and shallow, frightened breathing, as well as continued evidence of pain. 'What have you done so far?' he asked in an aside to Hayley.

Her short hair looked soft and feathery and her dark eyes bright, and if she'd been asleep in the stand-down room at ambulance headquarters when they'd been called out, you wouldn't have guessed. No creases, no rumples.

'Quite a lot,' she answered. 'Oxygen, ECG monitoring. That showed systolic elevation, strongly suggesting an AMI.' She used the accepted abbreviation for acute myocardial infarction. 'It was a typical presentation, as I said. Blood pressure was over 120 systolic so we were able to give morphine and he's reporting less pain.'

She named two more drugs they'd given him to get his heart working properly again, and Byron was impressed at how much she'd got through in a relatively short time.

'Trying to take over my job?' he teased her, feeling a tickle of curiosity as to how her smile withstood fatigue and disrupted biorhythms.

'Swap, if you like,' she came back at once, and it wasn't a smile at all, it was a grin. It had a mischievous, elfin quality, putting a twinkle in her dark eyes and wrinkling her nose just a little.

He felt warm and comfortable with her, and said on a sudden impulse, 'Hang around for a cup of tea, if Paul is willing.'

He marvelled at how effortless it was to take this small step towards reaching out, when for so long anything like that had required a tremendous rousing of his motivation.

'That'd be nice.' She nodded. 'Otherwise I'll go to sleep back at the station, and feel rotten when I have to wake up again in a couple of hours.' She yawned again, with a tidy fist over her generous mouth. 'Oh, excuse me!'

'No, I'll join you. It's contagious, isn't it?' He smothered a yawn of his own with his hand. They both laughed.

It took half an hour to get Mr Frewin stabilised and settled in the coronary care unit. Byron noted that Hayley's writing on the patient care report was as neat as her yawn.

Since he was the only doctor on duty now, he wasn't surprised to get called up to the maternity unit to check out a febrile baby, and that took a while. When he got back down to the A and E department, he found Hayley and Paul still drinking their tea and talking to the night nurse about favourite television shows, as if Hayley had taken his invitation as a general one rather than something personal from him to her.

Which made sense.

'Like another one?' he offered as she took a final gulp.

'Uh...will I?'

He waited, understanding that she was asking herself, not him.

She rolled her shoulders as if to get rid of a crick in her neck, and he was startled to find himself watching the way the crisp white shirt of her uniform pulled tighter across her neat, plump breasts as she pressed her arms back.

Lord, he was a mess, with this stuff! Noticing a woman's walk in the street was a far less disturbing phenomenon than feeling this sudden surge of desire for Hayley Morris. Both things were symptomatic of something he hadn't yet worked out how to tackle at all.

He'd taken a brief dinner break earlier and had dropped into Wendy's, arriving just minutes after she'd reached home herself. She'd still been wearing a pair of tight fawn jodhpurs and she'd smelled pungently of horse feed. She'd offered him a beer, which he'd turned down, and he'd handled the whole thing quickly but with dignity.

Or so he hoped, because if, in fact, he'd completely mangled the entire interview, Wendy wasn't the type to tell him so. She had looked a little surprised, but neither of them had lost face.

'It must be very hard,' Wendy had said, her words slower than usual in their sympathy.

The little spurt of guilt he'd felt made him wonder, for the first time, if this was as much about Elizabeth, and about him not being ready, as he'd thought. Oh, Lord, Wendy was right, it was hard! But perhaps not for the reasons she was imagining. He had left, feeling more uncomfortable than he should have done, given the well-bred way she'd reacted.

He was uncomfortable again now as he waited for Hayley's decision.

So I've abandoned a perfectly promising relationship with Wendy, only to start ogling the next unattached female who crosses my path? In addition to which, hadn't I already concluded that Hayley would be a big mistake? Was that a conclusion, actually, or simply another example of craven panic?

He wasn't looking for love—he couldn't—but were the alternatives any better?

'Paul, do you want one?' Hayley was saying to her partner.

'Can we head back? I'm not going to have another chance to get horizontal until tonight.'

'No worries. Look's like it's a no, Byron.'

She shrugged, and once more her breasts moved inside her shirt and he saw the pale shape of her bra. It felt…

Well, to revisit a dental analogy he'd used earlier, it felt as if his dentist had called him back, just when he'd thought he was safe for the next six months, to report a problem on the X-ray and announce a heavy schedule of essential root-canal treatment.

'I'll see you around, then,' he said to Hayley, adding to himself inwardly, Best if that's not too soon…

Perhaps we should have had it on a weekend,' said Tim Foster, the president of this year's preschool parents' committee.

He eyed Hayley and Byron, who eyed each other.

The three of them were the only people present at what was supposed to be a businesslike get-together of parent volunteers, with the purpose of repainting the preschool's play furniture and putting in some new garden beds.

'Or on a midweek night, rather than a Friday evening?' Byron suggested.

'Well, you know, we were going to have a Sausage Sizzle as well as the Working Bee,' Tim said, using two cheery expressions which every Australian parent of a school-age child soon learned to dread. 'We'd have drawn more volunteers that way because it would have been a social thing, but the Sausage Sizzle fell through.'

Hayley shifted her feet. The Sausage Sizzle had only fallen through because Tim had failed to deliver on his easy promise to track down a barbecue grill and get a notice out to parents. She had been to two preschool committee meetings now, in her self-inflicted role as fund-raising co-ordinator, and had formed the impression that their president wasn't going to be particularly efficient, this year. She could have got hold of a barbecue grill herself, only she'd thought that Tim had been doing it.

'With three of us, we've got two choices, I guess,' she said, trying to sound efficient, rather than merely bossy and impatient. 'We can either cancel now or scale down our ambitions.'

'Oh, let's not cancel,' Tim protested. 'Other people will show up. It's early days yet.'

'Five-thirty,' Byron murmured, after a glance at the plain silver watch on his wrist. The Working Bee had been scheduled to start at five, and he and Hayley had both turned up a little late themselves.

'Let's stick to the plan,' Tim said firmly. He had cans of paint, brushes, gardening tools, bags of soil and some old tractor tyres at the ready. 'We're going to repaint the play furniture and make some garden beds in these old tyres for the kids to plant things in. Why don't you two get stuck into the painting?' He gestured at the child-sized play furniture which was grouped on tarpaulins on the preschool lawn. 'I'll tackle the garden.'

'Sounds like a plan,' Byron said.

He glanced at his watch once more, then took it off, put it in his pocket and rolled up the sleeves of his thin and already paint-stained grey sweatshirt. His ancient jeans had paint all over them, too, and fitted tight across a masculine backside that could, Hayley suddenly discovered, have modelled denim at a professional level.

Hayley felt a little breathless and fluttery, as if she were fifteen again. Confused, too, about the sensation. Or perhaps the confusion was nothing to do with Byron himself—perhaps it had its source elsewhere. She'd been unsettled over the past few days.

Chris and Max had both still been sleeping when she'd got home from work last Saturday morning. She'd woken her ex-husband, thinking he'd want to make an early start back to Melbourne, but instead he'd tried to pull her into the bed with him—the same queen-sized bed they'd bought together during their marriage.

He had been warm and sleepy and already aroused, but she'd responded with both anger and impatience.

'Max is going to wake up any second, Chris.'

'Does that matter?'

'*Yes!* This is… We're divorced. You left.'

'I thought you wanted to be friends.'

'I don't sleep with my friends.'

'Maybe we wouldn't just be friends if we did.'

'What are you saying? That you definitely do want us to get back together?'

'I'm not saying anything, I'm just saying this feels nice. Does it have to be an either-or thing?'

'Yes! With our history, and with Max to consider, yes, it does!'

'Then it had better be no, I guess.' He added, muttering, 'There always has to be pressure, doesn't there?'

At this point, he rolled out of bed with his back to her, disappeared into the shower and left just five minutes after Max woke up. And, of course, she was left with the bitter taste of confusion and anger in her mouth, grittier and more uncomfortable than the dust Chris left in the air as he gunned his car down the dirt verge at the edge of her street before veering onto the road. Was she applying unfair pressure? Was she the one making it impossible for the two of them to work out what they wanted from each other?

'Have a brush,' Byron said, holding one out to her. 'This furniture is going to take longer than Tim thinks,' he added quietly.

'I know,' she agreed, glad that he could see it, too. 'But I guess we might as well do the whole job since we're here. Pointless to leave it half-finished when the kids will want to use it next week.'

Byron sat on his heels, making the fabric of his

jeans go taut across his strong thighs, and levered lids off paint with a screwdriver. The metal squawked. 'Looks like it's white with a blue trim.'

'Which bits are the trim?'

'Drawer handles? They unscrew, and it's the only way we'll get main colour and trim both done tonight. Let's not get too artistic or it'll take twice as long.'

'Or should we ask?'

They looked at Tim who was stalking around like a theatre director, assessing the placement of his tractor tyres from several angles.

'Let's make an executive decision,' Byron answered.

'The first of many, probably!'

He laughed, as if at a shared, gossipy secret. The sound was a short, rich gurgle, like a pebble dropping into a well, and there it was again, this little flutter inside her. She refused to examine it more closely, and focused instead on applying the glossy white paint smoothly and quickly.

'How's your mum, Byron?' she asked him.

'Progressing pretty well. In good spirits about everything, mostly. She gets down in the dumps on a day when I can't get there to see her, though.'

'So you do try to go every day?'

'If I possibly can.'

They talked about it a little more, and she got an even stronger sense of the caring she'd already seen in him.

After about fifteen minutes, Tim came over to inspect their work. 'Looks great.' He added a little too casually, 'Um, I need to head off. You know how to lock up, don't you, Hayley?'

'Yes, but—' She stood up, brush in hand.

'Keys are inside, by the sink. I'd better get away, because I'm late for another commitment. Great job, Byron, you'll knock it over by seven.'

Before they could say anything more, he loped out the gate, pulling his mobile phone from his pocket and giving them a last wave as he pressed it to his ear.

'Well!' Byron said.

'Did I miss something back there?'

'If you did, so did I. He didn't mention another commitment before. We can't possibly get this done by seven with just two of us.'

'We can forget the garden beds for tonight at least.'

'No, because he's opened all the bags of soil. It'll be easier to dump them in the tyres than carry them back to the shed. Then I suppose we should water it in...'

'Oh, good!'

'Do you know what I'm going to do?'

'Leave, too?' she suggested sweetly.

He laughed. 'No, so don't throw paint at me when you see me heading for my car, OK? I picked up some supplies today. Would you like a beer and some potato chips?'

'It would help!'

'If only I had a barbecue grill and some sausages, we could turn it into the originally intended social occasion.'

The beer was still cold from the supermarket fridge, and the chips were a spicy Bombay curry flavour, which made the beer taste both good and necessary. Byron even hunted up the preschool radio-cassette player and tuned it to a classic rock station, which played a steady stream of memory-evoking songs.

'Maybe I won't have to let down Tim Foster's car tyres after all,' Hayley decided darkly, after about fifteen minutes of working in silence together. 'This is nice.'

'That's the beer talking.'

'Wasn't that the point of having the beer?' she asked.

'To save Tim's tyres?'

'To make this nice.'

'Yes, it was,' he said. 'And it is. Where's Max tonight?'

'Oh, at Mum and Dad's.' She suppressed a sigh. 'I was supposed to be working, but Bruce asked me to swap shifts at short notice. He got the chance of a weekend's sailing and wanted to clear his schedule for tomorrow and Sunday. Max was already with Mum, so it didn't make sense to go and pick him up before morning, but I always feel guilty—I say always, but it doesn't happen very often—if I have them babysit for a reason other than work.'

'Guilty about overloading them, or about not spending enough time with Max?' Byron asked, zeroing in on the crucial issues at once.

'Both. I'd spend more time with him if I could. And,' she suddenly added on a rush, 'I feel angry with Chris for putting me in this position. For making it all such a struggle. I love what I do. The sense of being needed, of doing good work and, yes, the drama of it, too. But shift work as a single parent would be impossible without Mum and Dad.'

'It seemed as if you'd mended fences with Chris a bit the other day.'

'Yes. He decided to stay overnight after all, which helped. But then—' She stopped.

At the same moment, Byron accidentally flicked some paint onto his face. He hissed between his teeth. 'Damn!' and grabbed for a rag before it dribbled into his eye.

'Let me get it,' Hayley said. 'You can't tell where it is, and you'll only smear it.'

'Thanks.'

She put her paintbrush down and stood in front of him, taking the rag. He had paint in the crease of an eyelid and she instructed, 'You'll have to close your eyes.'

'What were you saying before?' he asked, as she dabbed at a smooth lid.

'Nothing, really.'

Silence. She felt the soft puff of his breath against her cheek. He looked very trusting and calm like this. Not distant and removed the way he sometimes did. Or not distant emotionally, at least. He was very tall, which gave him a physical distance even now, when they were standing very close. She had to reach up quite high.

His mouth was closed, firm, beautifully shaped. His jeans were soft against strong legs. Beyond the chemical smell of paint, she detected something tangy, musky and male.

'Oh, he just sent his usual mixed signals, that's all,' she went on, surprising herself.

It was a relief to say it to someone. Mum always got indignant and angry about Chris, and took

Hayley's side too willingly. Dad muttered murderous threats. She wanted support, of course, but didn't want to be made to feel that her ex-husband was completely worthless. He wasn't.

'What kind of mixed signals?' Byron wanted to know.

'That's got it all now,' she said absently, dropping the rag and picking up her brush again. 'Oh, you know, about the central issue—getting back together.'

'You'd like to?'

'I...don't know. I don't know how much I have the right to ask.'

She meant 'to ask of life'. Life didn't *owe* her a great love. People settled for what they could get, and for what was sensible. The fire faded and left...what? What she felt for Chris?

'So you're sending mixed signals, too?' Byron suggested. 'Maybe that makes sense of his.'

She laughed. 'Don't make it sound so simple!'

'It's always simpler when you look at it from an outsider's perspective,' he answered. 'I wish...' he sighed '...the stuff that I feel seemed simple.'

'About Elizabeth?' she questioned tentatively.

'*Is* it about Elizabeth? Or am I just hiding behind that? I— You know...probably you know...that I've been going out with Wendy Piper.'

'I'd heard,' she admitted cautiously. Felt tense suddenly. Just what, exactly, and how much, was she hoping to hear?

'Not any more,' he said.

'Is that a problem?' And why am I experiencing this rush of...?

'It was my decision. And it felt like such a relief.'

This rush of relief, Hayley echoed inwardly. That's the word.

'Only now…' Byron went on.

'You're lonely,' she guessed.

'Yes,' he answered.

'It's brutal, isn't it? It's an emotion that can really push you in bad directions. I *know* if I slept with Chris—'

Ouch! she realised. Didn't put it so bluntly to him before, did I? Talked about mixed signals. Vague and safe, before. Not any more. It was out in the open, quite stark.

'Yes, it might only be the prod of loneliness like a gun pressing into your back,' he finished for her. He didn't seem put off by her accidental confession. 'Hell, I know. I kept thinking that with Wendy, and then another part of me was saying, Do it anyway. Is there something wrong with wanting to assuage loneliness?'

'It's what happens afterwards that I'm worried about. With the history he and I have, it seems like he's not a safe person to make that sort of experiment with.'

'Yes, that makes sense…'

It was the kind of conversation they never could have had while facing each other over a meal, or even sitting on a cliff top watching waves pounding on the rocks. But with their hands busy, and their eyes forced to look elsewhere, and just enough of their minds occupied by the tasks of brushing glistening paint onto well-loved planes of wood, everything they said to each other was natural and unthreatening and right.

Gradually, it began to get dark, and they turned on

the lights inside the preschool so that they flooded through the glass of the floor-to-ceiling windows and it was still possible to see what they were doing. It was a mild night, so the paint would dry without blistering.

Byron took another beer. Hayley had enough sense to keep to one bottle, but then she absent-mindedly took some gulps from his and didn't realise until she found her own bottle where she'd originally left it, beside a tin of paint, with just one mouthful left in it.

She flicked a quick glance across at him, to see if he'd noticed, and found that he'd picked up the bottle himself and was drinking from it with his throat stretched and his head tipped back, his mouth falling exactly where she'd had hers not sixty seconds earlier. His fingers were wrapped smooth and strong around the cold glass of the bottle.

There was no reason for it to be a significant thing, but somehow it was. Hadn't she read once that if two people drank from the same place, their lives would be linked from then on? The seductive appeal of the idea disturbed her. Despite their easy conversation tonight, she knew, from his own lips, how much of his soul was still locked away inside his grief for his lost marriage.

When he put the beer bottle down, he said drily, 'You know, I don't think anyone else is coming.'

She laughed. 'You're Sherlock Holmes with that brilliant deduction.'

They finished the painting at a quarter to eight, and spent another fifteen minutes rinsing brushes and tidying up. Most of the furniture was already touch-dry and they could bring it inside. The final pieces soon would be.

'Let's tackle those tyres,' Byron said. 'At least we don't actually have to do the planting tonight.'

'There's a full moon coming up,' Hayley observed. 'Aren't there some kinds of seeds you're supposed to plant by the light of the full moon?'

'Parsley, I think, and only if you want to get pregnant,' Byron tossed casually back.

He heard the words hanging in the air in a far too significant way.

It was a relief to him when Hayley laughed, and the fact that she was looking down very intently at the bag of soil she was about to lift couldn't mean anything. He had been aware of her ever since she'd stood so close to him to wipe the paint from his face. No, be honest, he'd been aware of her from the moment she'd arrived here tonight, five minutes after he had.

She was wearing a snug-fitting purple T-shirt and a pair of cut-off jeans that finished with a frayed edge at the tops of her thighs. Her legs were as smooth and brown as gingerbread dough. He knew that gingerbread dough was the right comparison because Monica and Tori had made some yesterday, and he'd been generously invited to lick the spoon. Today, Monica had taken Tori up to Canberra for two nights to visit some old friends, and he was aware of his empty house like—yes, back to the dental similes— a dully aching tooth.

'I must make an appointment to get my teeth checked,' he muttered to himself. 'My subconscious is obviously trying to tell me something.'

Only it probably wasn't about his teeth...

'I'm sorry?' Hayley said brightly. She'd tipped her bag of soil into the first of the tyres.

'Just wondering if I need a filling replaced,' he answered, stumbling over the words a little. Heavens, he'd had less than two beers!

'Oh, you have a hurting tooth?'

'Mmm.'

'If you need to get home...' she offered bravely. Had she thought he was lining up an excuse?

'Do you think for a second that I'd leave you here to finish by yourself?' he growled.

To prove his point, he hefted two bags of soil into the tyres in the time it took her to do one, and they used up all the bags quite quickly. He had time, as he worked, to appreciate the snug fit of her shorts, and the way those frayed edges rode up a little at the back when she bent to shake the soil out of a bag. Not a distant appreciation, like the kind he'd felt for women in the street, not an abstract hormonal pull of male need, but a very specific, very powerful desire for Hayley Morris and Hayley Morris alone.

Bending did other delicious things to her body as well, he noted next. It made her hair fall against her face in a clean, glossy curtain. It emphasised the neat tuck of her waist and made her breasts bounce with generous weight.

'They're too full,' she said, stepping back.

No, they're not, they're just right.

Aaghh! What was wrong with him? She was talking about the dirt heaped inside the tyres. He gathered his wits with difficulty.

'It'll compact down once we water it in,' he said. 'Is there a hose, or will we have to use buckets?'

'There's a hose in the shed.' She went to find it while he carried the last of the touch-dry painted furniture inside and gathered up the tarpaulins.

'Found it!' he heard her call from the shed's crowded depths.

'If there's a shovel as well,' he said, coming through the shed door, 'you can spray and I can—'

'Oops!' she gasped.

It wasn't a full-on collision, but close. Byron had to put his hands on her shoulder and waist to steady them both, and he briefly felt the soft push of one of those delicious breasts against his ribs. Every nerve-ending in his body sprang to attention, and blood rushed to his head...and to other places. Beneath the thin, snug T-shirt and soft bra, he couldn't help noticing that her nipples had hardened in response. Him? His nearness? Or was she just getting cold?

'Sorry,' she blurted. 'This hose is making me clumsy.'

And you, Hayley, are making me...

Crawl. Pulse. Ache. Dream.

He fought it all back. No dental analogies this time. He just fought it, afraid of the power of his need, disturbed at how much he wanted to read into her own unconscious reaction.

It had been far too long. Far, far too long. He wanted to end the drought that his grief had imposed, but... What had she said herself, tonight, in relation to Chris? 'The right person to make that kind of experiment with.'

Right now, his body was urging him that Hayley

was *exactly* the right person. She was here. She was female. Just how finicky did he have to be?

'Let's shower some cold…' No. *He* was the one that needed the cold shower. He tried again. 'Let's spray on the water and get out of here.' Once more, it came out on a growl. 'We've spent long enough on this. Who on earth voted Tim as president, anyway?'

'He was the only one who volunteered.'

'Now, why does that sound familiar, I wonder?' he muttered grimly.

'Mmm.' She looked a little tense and uncomfortable at the sudden darkening of his mood.

He took the hose from her and attached it to the tap near the sand-pit. She laid out its coils and stood ready beside the tyres. He turned on the water, then found the shovel in the shed and used the back of it to spread and flatten the dampened dirt.

It went fine until Hayley accidentally caught him with a tickling spray of water, then suddenly they both just completely lost it.

'Hey!' he protested, then laughed as he straightened to glare at her and saw her exaggerated wince and apologetic grin. 'Actually, thanks! It's nice,' he added, subtly daring her.

It was a mild evening, they'd worked hard and the water felt refreshing on his neck and shoulder. She responded to his dare, squirting the spray at him again, on the chest this time. 'Accident, sorry,' she claimed with a straight face.

'Right…' he drawled.

Byron knew she was lying. Her face gave too much away. He read relief at the easing of his recent tension and a mischievous temptation as to which way to take this. OK, then…

He flicked a small lump of soil in her direction and it shattered against the front of her T-shirt. She sprayed his face. He found another lump of dirt, feinted a throw to distract her and used his chance to seize the hose.

Dear God, how long had it been since he'd laughed like this, and for such a reason? It was insane, childish, hedonistic. She was shrieking, he was yelling. Soon they were completely covered in mud and tussling like battling soldiers for the hose. The mud smelt fresh and rich after the unpleasant fumes of the paint. Muddy water was streaming down the slope of lawn and into the bushes, and if anyone had happened to be passing…

'Hayley, stop!' he begged breathlessly.

'Make me!'

'I will…' he threatened.

He didn't give her time to react, just threw all good sense to the four winds and did what he'd been wanting to do all evening—what even the half erotic, half uncomfortable sublimation of dirt and water hadn't been able to distract him from thinking about for long.

He wrapped his arms around her, while the hose continued to gush forgotten in the grass, bent his head and kissed her fresh, wet lips with a hunger whose consequences, for once, he didn't even begin to consider.

CHAPTER FIVE

OH, IT felt so good! They'd both known, hadn't they? Two grown professionals didn't pelt each other with dirt and fight to spray each other with cold water just because it was a Friday night and they'd been stuck together, against their will, after a long week, painting the preschool furniture.

Hayley had sensed the building awareness between them from the moment she'd tasted Byron's beer. No, earlier. Much earlier. Weeks ago, the day Tori had been burned.

Or, at least, that was how it seemed now, in his arms. As if she *must* have known, because this was too powerful to have come upon her only recently and without warning.

She heard her own moan of delight like some primitive, magical chorus, emphasising the fact that there was nothing civilised about this. Earlier there had been. Discoursing to each other about the complex legacies of their respective marriages had been very civilised indeed. Modern in the best sense, suggesting as it did the sort of openness and equality a man and a woman could achieve together these days.

This, though…

His mouth was cold on hers at first, and his nose, bumping against her cheek, was wet. His thin sweater was cold, too, and clung to every contour of his well-muscled chest and arms. Soon, however, she felt the warmth of the body beneath, and the tang of his fresh beer taste. There was a tiny nuance of mud in the mix as well.

He kissed so cleanly and with such relish and heat. His mouth was firm and hard, but beyond his parted lips there was a sweetness and softness that made seductive promises about where else he would press those lips, what other parts of her body he would make sing with the caress of his tongue. Something clenched and shuddered inside her.

The way their wet clothes clung to them, they might as well have been naked. Cold made everything firmer, tighter. Her nipples were like gemstones, and it didn't take him long to discover the fact. His hands, already warmed from pressing against the contours of her waist, thrust up inside her T-shirt and covered her breasts, thumbing their peaks through her soft bra with slow, circular movements.

Hayley strained against him, wanting more, wishing that she were naked, and that they were anywhere but here. She slid her hands into the back pockets of his jeans and held on for dear life, didn't even realise how firmly she was anchoring his arousal against her, or what erotic friction she was applying there, until she felt him shudder and pull back.

'There's no shower here?' he asked urgently.

'No.' She slid her hands out of his pockets, her heart pounding hard and slow.

'No bed either. Hayley, I want more than this.'

'Yes. Me, too.'

Byron's blunt statement and her equally blunt reply were both charged with the power of their need. Saying it felt like doing it.

'There's probably all sorts of stuff we should be saying to—'

'Please, let's not. I'm so sick of *talking* about, oh, everything. But we do have to—'

'Lock up the preschool. Shut off this wretched—'

'I guess we should be grateful to Tim, though, really.' She laced her fingers loosely behind Byron's head and laughed. He had streaks of mud on his nose and rivulets of brown-stained water running down from his hair. He looked alive and happy and gorgeous, and as if his existence were utterly carefree.

'Oh, it would have happened anyway,' he growled, holding her hips.

'W-would it?' His casual certainty made her more breathless than ever.

'Hell, yes! One way or another. I hope you won't take this the wrong way, Hayley, but I *need* this. Tonight. Now. With you, and no one else but you. I'll do the hose. You lock up. Then—Monica and Tori are away—we're going to my place and we're going to bed. At least, that's if—'

He let her go abruptly, and she could almost hear the screeching sound of the brakes he had applied to his urgent need. His dark gaze burned into hers, his lids narrowing his eyes to slits and a frown scribbled on his brow like an angry child's drawing. He wasn't angry, though, she knew. Just belatedly wondering if he'd come on too strong.

He hadn't.

'Yes. It's fine, Byron. I...' she took a shuddering breath '...need it, *want* it, as much as you do.'

'Good!' Water glistened on his neck, and he wiped the back of his hand across his mouth, leaving another streak of mud on his cheek. The open awareness of desire was like a force dragging on their bones.

They didn't waste another second. He grabbed the hose, twisted the nozzle shut, then coiled it up as he went towards the tap. Hayley surveyed the muddy mess they'd left and gave a mental shrug. Most of the dirt was still where it belonged. That grassy slope got muddy in the rain anyway. They hadn't done any damage. No one would guess that if this had been a hot summer night, they might easily have made love right here in the mud they'd made.

Byron gathered the empty plastic dirt bags and wadded them into the garbage bin while Hayley locked the shed, turned off the lights and locked the building. They walked in silence to their respective cars and he delivered one very husky 'See you at my place' before sliding into the plush upholstered driver's seat of his car.

Knowing more than he did about the mud on the taut backside of his jeans, Hayley winced, then defiled her own car in a similar manner. As if it mattered, when all she could think of was what lay ahead. She followed his taillights hungrily as they drove, as if she were in danger of getting lost.

'Cold?' he asked, as they hurried through the court-yard and up his front steps a few minutes later.

'Yes.'

'Shower, then.'

It seemed as if they were both reduced to mono-syllables, or at most a simple phrase. The last thing Hayley wanted was to talk. They'd already talked to-night, for a long time. She'd spent years talking with Chris, back and forth, about their problems. She didn't want that with Byron. Didn't want to second-guess tonight in any way. It was happening. They wanted it. They trusted each other, respected each other, and there was nothing in their casual, comradely history to flag a warning against doing so. That was all that mattered right now.

His shower was as gorgeous as he was. Fully glassed-in and huge, it was set at an angle to the rest of the spacious bathroom, and jutted out into its own tiny and completely private courtyard, which was already planted with lush, moisture-loving ferns and rainforest greenery. Byron didn't light the bathroom itself, just flicked a switch to illuminate the courtyard, then turned and bathed her in his hot gaze as he pulled her T-shirt upwards over her head, then reached around to unfasten her bra.

He kissed her neck and she arched her throat back with a tiny shudder. 'You taste like mud,' he muttered.

'So do you. You could lick it off...'

'I will.'

Her breasts were cold and tight, and her hands were eager to undress him. But Byron hadn't waited. The sweater was already off, so she curled her fingers over the damp waistband of his jeans instead, then slid them around to his sides as he tore open snap and fly. He reached into the shower alcove and turned on a wide, strong jet of water with one hand, dragging down his jeans with the other. They kicked off shoes and underwear impatiently, then stepped into the steamy enclosure together.

With the subtly floodlit greenery outside, it was like showering under a jungle waterfall, except that the water was hot and generous on their chilled skins and the air was filled with steam. For a solid minute, the water ran muddy brown through the drain hole and Hayley murmured, 'I never realised we were that much of a mess.'

'It's in your hair, too. Close your eyes.'

He splayed his fingers and pulled her head into the streaming water. She felt the cool pooling of some fragrant shampoo. He massaged the mud from her scalp, then heaped her hair on top of her head while he cleaned mud from her neck and behind her ears, his fingertips moving in slow, caressing circles.

'Mmm…' She swayed, eyes still closed and going limp with pleasure. It was a sensual massage, teasing and promising, and a moment later she felt the wet brush of his mouth on hers and the whisper of his hands on her breasts. With her head beneath the water again, the lather cascaded down over her body in a warm, tickling wave.

She shuddered, managed to drag her eyes open and reach for his hair to give it the same treatment. He was so tall! It gave her a delicious and unashamedly selfish sense of power to pull him down within her reach, and when she'd rinsed his hair clean he took advantage of their position, bent his head lower and brushed his lips across one eager nipple, then the other.

'Bed,' he said.

'Wet?'

'No, of course not.'

Towels. Huge, fluffy, fresh. They dried each other, seriously intent on the task, making fresh discoveries about each other's bodies through the thick towelling.

'I was sick of being wet,' she said.

'So was I. Fun until a minute ago, but...' He threw the towels back on the heated rail, took her hand to lead her to his king-sized bed, and enfolded them both in a heavy, down-filled doona instead. 'Still cold?' he asked.

'A bit.'

'I'll warm you.'

She hadn't expected it—that he could just hold her, so still and close. No caresses for now. A brief respite from their shared impatience. It shouldn't have been half as arousing as it was. Then he began to move his hands, and she knew what arousal really was.

This.

This intoxicating mix of satisfaction and ever-increasing need. This sense that every touch of skin on skin was miraculous. Selfishness one minute as she anchored his head between her breasts and demanded the continuing bliss of his mouth, generosity the next as she raked her nails lightly down his back, over his flat, muscled stomach, across his tight male nipples, and felt him shudder and groan.

He asked her an urgent question about protection and she answered with just as much impatience, 'I'm on the Pill. I just...sort of...never stopped taking it.'

There was a tiny silence as they both registered what this said about her uncertainty regarding Chris, then they let it go and forgot everything but each other.

Hayley was as greedy for Byron's pleasure as she was for her own, and finally, when their release came in bouts of rippling waves like boat wake surging onto a beach, she could hardly distinguish between his climax and hers.

Neither of them spoke for a long time. There was something...*humbling* about what they'd just shared. Chatty conversation, or even ords of thanks or compliments to each other would have seemed impossibly thin and shallow. Instead, they said everything through touch.

He gave her a hard, strong squeeze, which she returned in full. Then his limbs relaxed and he caressed her, softly and lazily. Her hair, her breasts, her thighs. She kissed him in return, pressed her lips to his temple and his jaw, buried her face in the fragrant curve of his neck and shoulder, stroked his hard, hair-roughened thigh.

When he finally did speak, his voice sounded creaky, like an old gate gone stiff from disuse.

'Do you remember, oh, about a hundred years ago, earlier tonight, you said something about Chris not being a safe person for you to experiment with?'

'Mmm, I remember.'

It was the point at which she'd confessed a lot more to Byron than she'd intended. She waited, now, for a wash of regret about her honesty, but it didn't come. She appreciated the way he'd reacted to what she'd said—had *needed* to say to someone—about her life, her needs, her uncertain feelings.

'Would you...be interested in making the experiment with me, instead?'

'Sleeping together,' she clarified, though he could hardly have been talking about anything else.

They were still bathed in its aftermath. She felt

physically unable to move, and mentally too...lazy, perhaps, to even think about it.

'We already have, haven't we?' she said.

'Yes, but I'm talking about something more like an ongoing, open-ended affair.'

'I know you are. I'm sorry. I'm making this hard.'

'No, *I'm* sorry. Perhaps it's a very narrowly defined proposition, just an affair, but I...have to be honest. I can't offer anything else.' His voice was suddenly heavy, tired, almost distant. 'The totality that most women—and really, when they're honest, most men—are looking for, I mean. I couldn't...wouldn't even *want* to...offer that again, but I need this. And if by some chance—Well, tonight seemed to suggest that you need it, too.'

'Yes. I...hadn't actually looked at it that way before, but perhaps you're right. It would be disastrous if I let Chris back into my life purely because I was—'

'Sex-starved?' he offered.

'Sex-starved,' she repeated crisply. 'Thank you.'

'Sorry, that was a bit too—'

'No, but it fits.' Her brief irritation evaporated as suddenly as it had come. 'It's the word. You can get into a lot of trouble if you don't call feelings by their proper names. And I do need to find the proper name for what I feel about Chris.'

And about Byron? That thought evaporated, too, even before it was fully formed.

'To hell with Chris!' he said suddenly, and rolled so that she was pinned beneath his naked hips, with his body weight supported on his elbows and the muscles of his upper arms and chest hard and tight. His chest was gorgeous from this angle. She flattened her palms against it, felt the light roughness of hair, then his mouth came down to sear across hers. 'To hell with anything but this! It was amazing. I want more of it. With you. Think about it, and if it's the same for you, can we, please?'

'Can we, please, what?' she said foolishly, biding her time or perhaps seeking clarity.

Both of which were suddenly, a moment later, unnecessary.

'I thought I'd made that very clear,' he growled in reply. His hands grazed the sides of her breasts. 'Didn't I?'

'Yes. Yes, you did,' she admitted, her stomach lurching with freshened desire. 'It was amazing for me, too.'

It wasn't quite the agreement he had so confidently demanded, but he took it as such, and this time when he kissed her he didn't stop for a long time.

'Are you staying tonight?'

Hell, soften it a bit, can't you? Byron chided himself. He'd sounded gruff, blunt, casual.

It was late, and they had just finished eating. He'd been ravenous. Well, it was eleven o'clock, and they'd had only chips and beer at the preschool, hours ago. He'd made piles of ham and tomato sandwiches and grilled cheese on toast, and a big pot of tea, and they'd finished with strawberries freshly sliced over ice cream and mugs of hot chocolate.

Because Hayley's recently muddy and sodden clothes were still in his clothes dryer, he'd lent her some of his—a navy blue V-necked T-shirt, which was huge on her and kept sliding seductively off her shoulder, and a pair of navy silk boxer shorts with red polka dots. These had been a Christmas gift from his sister in London, and he wished he could see more of them beneath the dress-length hem of the T-shirt.

Curled up on his forest green leather couch, still finishing her hot chocolate, Hayley hesitated at his too-blunt question, but didn't seem to resent it.

'Um, well, I usually pick Max up straight after the end of my shift. Mum knows I'm not working after all, but she'll still expect me pretty early. I'd hate her to…worry.'

Or suspect.

Byron understood that clearly, although he didn't say it and neither did she. He felt the same. He didn't want Monica to know about this. She was leaving on Wednesday, taking the bus to Sydney then flying back to Brisbane, and despite his fondness for her he was looking forward to her departure now. If she met Hayley, guessed what had begun between them and reacted the way she'd reacted to Wendy Piper…

He suddenly realised that her opinion, although it might make him feel awkward, wouldn't influence his actions. He would keep on seeing Hayley, sleeping with her, no matter what anyone else thought, and if their affair ended, it would only be because one or both of them wanted it to. His almost ruthless certainty about this was like a series of iron injections after a bout of anaemia. There wasn't much he'd felt certain about over the past few years.

It seemed to confirm what he and Hayley had both said, and felt, about calling things by their correct names. This wasn't a panicky quest to find a mother substitute for Tori, a second marriage that his heart didn't remotely want. This was about his own needs, right now, about learning to live again, about moving on, as far as that was possible.

'What time do you normally get to your parents' place?' he asked.

'Barring a late finish, about six-thirty.' Her answer was as practical and to the point as his question.

'We'll set the alarm,' he suggested.

She stilled, with the mug of hot chocolate held halfway to her mouth. 'So you want me to stay?'

'Yes. Very much.'

'I was…offering you a way out just now, you realise.'

'I don't need one. Stay. If *you* want to.'

'I do.' She looked at him with newly pink cheeks and added, very deliberately, the phrase he'd finished with. 'Very much.'

Then she put down her mug, stood up and came towards him with her need and desire written so clearly on her face that he was shaking before he took a single step to meet her. Dear Lord, on a physical level there was nothing distant or confused about this at all! The silk boxer shorts, warm from her skin beneath, felt as slippery and delicious in his hands as he'd imagined they would, and the shape of her was so lush and female that he just couldn't let go.

He carried her all the way to the bedroom.

They forgot to set the alarm, but it didn't matter. Hayley hardly slept, and encountered the red numbers on the clock-radio by Byron's bed every time she opened her eyes—2.15…4.25…6.03.

She didn't even try to sleep after that. Just lay with Byron's strong chest against her back and his hand resting, heavy and warm and relaxed, over her hip. She could feel his breathing tangling in the loose hair at the back of her neck and she could hear the rhythm of it, too, as a softer counterpoint to the sigh and wash of the ocean, less than a hundred metres away.

It didn't feel real, to be lying here beside him like this. There was a tiny part of her that still felt fifteen years old, that still saw him as cute, tanned B.J. from swim club. Mostly, though, it was nothing to do with any of that, and they weren't adolescents any more. The thing she couldn't stop thinking about was how much of a sheer *treat* it was to lie beside a man after so many nights of loneliness, so many nights wrapped in tears and anger and hurt, instead of warm male arms.

But now, for the time being at least, she had to end it.

With a reluctance so strong it was like overcoming paraplegia, she reached down and gently lifted Byron's big, warm hand from her hip. Sliding across the sheets, she knew she had begun to awaken him and was very tempted to slide back again, touch her mouth to his and take advantage of the moment.

But she knew she couldn't. Max would soon be up and about. Mum deserved a break, since she'd be taking him tonight as well. Then, blessedly, Hayley had two more days off…

Her stomach rolled suddenly.

I want to spend them with Byron. In bed. Eating and laughing. Not thinking. Not even talking much.

But, my Lord, how on earth are we going to manage it?

He'd talked about not thinking too far ahead. All well and good, but at the moment she couldn't even see how this affair of theirs was going to make it beyond today.

'You look tired, love,' Adele Kennett told her daughter. 'I thought you didn't have to work last night after all.'

'Just had a bad night,' Hayley answered, glad that she had her back to her mother while she filled the kettle at the kitchen sink for coffee.

She knew that her eyelids were creased and papery, and they felt as if they had beach sand stuck beneath them. She couldn't help wondering, as well, whether Byron's love-making had marked her in some way. Surely it had! Her mouth felt softer and fuller than usual. Her breasts throbbed subtly. Every joint felt loose and sinuous and replete.

'Have you heard from Chris?'

The timing of the question suggested that Adele thought Hayley had been lying awake thinking about her ex-husband.

And I was, I suppose, for part of the time.

A tiny part. The rest of the night, though…

'Yes, he phoned a few nights ago,' she answered brightly. 'He couldn't work out the different forms for all the new tax stuff.'

'Don't do it for him. You've got enough on your plate.'

'I know, but—'

'Send him to an accountant. It's not your problem.

It hasn't been your problem for more than three years.'

'Mum…'

'Oh, I know, you hate it when I say this, but—'

'Would you want us to be so hostile we couldn't exchange a civil word?' Still at the sink, wiping up a spill Max had made when he'd tried to pour his own juice, she threw the question over her shoulder. 'He's Max's father. It has to be better for all three of us if Chris and I can stay friends.'

'He's using you.'

'Yes, and I let it happen with my eyes open, for Max's sake. It's not a huge thing.'

'Just for Max's sake?'

'Hey, you said I should come in for breakfast, not for an interrogation session!' Head down, she scrubbed furiously at a spotless sink.

Then she felt her mother's arms slide warmly around her waist. 'I can't help it, love, when you deserve so much better. I'm your mother.'

She turned into those familiar arms, and brushed her cheek against her mother's temple.

'Can you leave it, then?' she said. 'I'm working things out, slowly, and I think Chris is starting to grow up. I mean, he actually stayed overnight last week, didn't he? Instead of driving straight back. Because he could see I was worried. He'd never have done that three years ago. He'd have jumped straight into his car just to prove a point, just to win.'

'Is that what you're waiting for? Is that what you're counting on? For him to grow up enough to…?' Mum sounded alarmed, and not happy.

'I—I don't know, Mum.' Hayley paused, then

added slowly, 'You know, when we were married I never realised you disliked him so much.'

'I don't dislike him. I don't. But he hurt you and… you know, a mother is like a lioness.'

Hayley looked at the short and slightly plump, grey-haired figure standing so close. Mum was wearing bifocal glasses, fluffy sheepskin slippers, Wedgwood blue sweatpants with a matching floral top, and a lime green apron patterned with citrus fruits.

Deliberately, Hayley tilted her head to one side and murmured, 'A lioness. Of course. Why didn't I see it before?'

Mum batted her forearm with a playful, lioness-like slap. 'You know what I mean. Forgive me, OK? And be careful!'

'I will. I am.'

I'm sleeping with someone else, a man I'm enormously attracted to, trust absolutely, and who can't and won't promise anything more than an open-ended affair.

Was that being careful? In hindsight, creaky with fatigue and standing in her mother's sunny morning kitchen, it seemed like the height of recklessness and folly.

Until she was engulfed by a sudden sense memory of last night…Byron's body tangled with hers, his hands and mouth discovering the secret places in her body…and she realised that the recklessness of it didn't matter. Perhaps it was even part of the attraction. To feel such a strong, simple and unquestioning rush of feeling. To embrace something new, without compromise. To be doing it for herself, not for anyone else.

Max ran into the kitchen at that moment, fully dressed, T-shirt on backwards, and ready for breakfast. Hayley welcomed the distraction. She bent down and scooped him up in her arms.

'Hi, gorgeous. Do you see what you've done with your shirt?'

He looked down and giggled. 'Oops!'

'Shall we fix it?'

'You fix it.'

'OK, up arms, then.' She gathered the T-shirt at his neck and pivoted it a hundred and eighty degrees. Max fought his arms back into it and pulled it down.

'Are you making pancakes, Grandma?'

'No, just toast today. Or cereal with banana.'

'Cereal with banana,' he echoed, and the day settled into a familiar, comfortable routine.

On the surface, anyway.

To be honest, it was anything *but* comfortable inside Hayley's head. After breakfast, she took Max home and they did weekend jobs together. Laundry, cleaning, some grocery shopping, a little bit of work in the garden, which fortunately was small and didn't require a lot of time. They had lunch and watched a children's video together, then spent a couple of hours on the beach.

When the phone rang, though, Hayley immediately thought, Byron!

At the supermarket in the morning, she'd looked for him as she turned down every aisle, and when Max had asked in the afternoon which beach they should go to and had listed their usual local favour-

ites, she'd come out with a studied casualness that
would have had her mother instantly on the alert, 'No,
how about we try North Moama for a change?'

That was, of course, the beach directly across from
Byron's house.

They hadn't seen him. He'd probably been working, gardening, shopping, visiting his mother at the
rehab centre. And, of course, it wasn't him on the
phone, just some polling organisation wanting
Hayley's opinion on a series of household products
that she never used.

After the beach, she'd popped Max into the bath to
wash off sand and salt and had made a chicken casserole to take to her parents' that night. It was something she did at least twice a week, despite her
mother's protests. It was an ongoing tussle between
them, with Hayley attempting to repay her parents for
all the help they gave, and her mum and dad doing
their best to give her even more.

Already wearing a clean uniform, she dropped Max
and the casserole at her parents' house at twenty to
six, then spent the next two hours wondering if Byron
was rostered at the hospital that night. She found out
at about eight-thirty, after they'd been called to a pale
green house in one of Arden's older streets, where an
elderly woman had fallen down the front step and was
in considerable pain.

The signs pointed to a fractured hip, a common
problem in old age, and it wasn't good news. The
fracture signalled a major loss of mobility in the future. Hayley started the patient on oxygen, took her
observations and hooked her up to the ECG monitor.
She wanted to administer morphine, and needed to

keep an eye on blood pressure and heart rhythm to check that the elderly patient was tolerating the drug's depressive effect on her system. Apparently she'd had heart trouble in the past.

It was Wendy Piper, not Byron Black who met them at the ambulance bay outside A and E, and the level of Hayley's disappointment gave her a sudden and unexpected jolt of something that felt like vertigo. How quickly could a casual affair go from being nice to being necessary? she wondered. And where did it go after that?

She handed over to Wendy, who wasn't optimistic when she'd heard the details.

'She's ninety-three,' Wendy murmured. 'It's the beginning of the end. I think she senses it, too…'

As Hayley was climbing back into Car seven, the patient's daughter rushed up to her, very emotional.

'Thank you,' she said. 'Thank you so much! She didn't even want to come in at first. Do you know when she'll be able to get back home?'

'That's up to her doctor, and it depends on how she progresses from now on,' Hayley said gently. 'I hope it isn't too difficult for her.'

They got called out twice more, both of them incidents related to Saturday night and alcohol. At ten o'clock, a teenager unused to drinking had passed out and panicked his friends, and at eleven-thirty they were called to what they and the police both knew was a domestic dispute, although the injured woman, washed-out and nervous, claimed, 'Silly me! I slipped in the bathroom and my face hit the tub. I don't remember anything after that until I saw Dave bending over me.'

'Thash right,' her husband added at once. 'Thash what happened. She doesn't remember a th-thing.' He'd obviously been drinking. 'But she's fine now.'

'They'll want to take a look at you in hospital, Mrs Murphy,' Paul said.

'I'm fine. Dave panicked, that's all.'

'Just in case. You probably are fine, but if you passed out for a bit, they like to make sure.'

'All right.' She glanced sideways at her husband. 'I suppose it can't hurt.'

Hayley put a cryptic comment in her notes to alert the medical staff to the need to talk to the patient about local support services, but Paul growled to her quietly in the car, 'She already knows what's available. This has been going on for years. I've seen her at least three times. She said something once… I think she's waiting till the kids leave home, which should be pretty soon now.'

'Still, it doesn't hurt to repeat it,' Hayley said. 'You never know at what point she'll be ready to leave.'

'No, that's true,' he agreed. 'Let's hope for the best. I have to keep my hands behind my back sometimes, with men like him!'

I wish we were handing over to Byron…

Hayley couldn't help thinking that way, although when she examined how she was feeling she decided it was selfish. Mrs Murphy would probably much prefer to be treated by a woman.

There wasn't a lot she could do for the patient in the car, but she took down more detail about what Mrs Murphy said had happened, and the last thing she could remember. The story was vague and inconsistent, and finally the woman admitted, almost inaudibly, 'Dave pushed me. That's how I fell.' She put a hand over her eyes.

'It's all right, Mrs Murphy,' Hayley told her. 'Think about what you want to do and, please, ask at the hospital if there's anyone you want to talk to about it.'

By the time she lay down to catch a brief few hours' sleep in the stand-down room, Hayley was tired and unsettled inside. She slept restlessly and dreamed erotically, and the man in her dreams was Byron.

CHAPTER SIX

'LISTEN, are you busy this morning?' Byron said quietly to Hayley on Thursday morning. There was a little burr in his voice that she found delicious with its suggestion of a shared secret.

They were both kneeling on the floor of the preschool, surrounded by four-year-olds, parents and puzzles, and both were casually dressed. Hayley wore jeans and a buttoned cotton cardigan, while Byron was dressed in navy canvas trousers and a grey-blue shirt.

'No, I'm not busy,' she answered. She knew at once what he meant. She'd thought of it as soon as she'd seen him come in, holding Tori's hand. Not Monica. Not Tori's day-care mother, Robyn. Byron himself. If that meant he wasn't working this morning... 'But what about Monica?'

'She left yesterday. I, uh, swapped rosters with someone else, on the off chance, hoping I'd worked out where you were up to in your shift rotation.'

'On the off chance?' she echoed, before she could stop herself.

'I know. Sounds a bit desperate, doesn't it?'

The easy admission from him made her laugh, and did something to her insides at the same time.

'I'm not busy,' she said, her voice breathy and low.

'Good. Meet me, then?'

'Your place?'

'Sounds good.'

'Mummy, you're not helping!' Max protested. For a child who usually preferred to do everything himself, this was uncharacteristic.

He's picked up a vibe, Hayley realised.

Had Karen, too? She came over and bent down to them. 'Tim says you're the ones I should thank for our beautiful furniture and garden. It's disappointing we didn't get a better turn-out at the Working Bee on Friday.'

'We enjoyed it more than we expected to,' Byron answered very seriously. 'Didn't we, Hayley?'

She fought a terrible urge to giggle, and managed to affirm, 'Yes, it was fun, in the end. Neither of us had anything else planned for the evening.'

Neither of us would have dared to plan what had actually happened…

'Well, thanks anyway,' Karen said. 'I'm afraid it always tends to be the same few parents who do all the work.'

She moved away to speak to another mother, and Tori grabbed her father's arm. 'You can go now, Daddy. See? The other parents are.'

'Right, yes,' he answered gravely.

'You're not supposed to stay past puzzle time unless you're on roster.'

'OK. You've got the timetable all worked out, haven't you?'

'It's easy,' she said airily. 'We have group time now, then activities.'

'Have fun. Do me a painting.'

'No, I'm doing a painting for Granny Black today.'

Max wasn't as loquacious in saying goodbye, so

Hayley and Byron walked out of the preschool together, rather self-conscious in their avoidance of conversation and positioned well apart. They reached his place in five minutes.

'Um,' Byron said as he unlocked the front door. 'Does it feel different in the daylight? The other night was—'

'The other night was everything we said it was at the time,' she answered, not as calm as she was pretending to be. 'It's fine. This *is* going to be different, but just as good.'

'We've got about three hours.'

'We should have asked Tori to give us a timetable.' The joke was a bit wobbly and didn't quite come off.

He still hadn't fully opened the front door. Instead, he was leaning on the handle and twisting to face her, while she rested the palm of her hand at head level on the wall of the house. The morning sun was bright in their faces, and the sound of the ocean was loud. Byron had to squint a little. Or maybe it wasn't the sun that was screwing up his face.

'A swim first?' he suggested. 'Would that be…?'

Another sentence unfinished.

'Haven't you ever had an affair before?' she teased.

'No,' he answered seriously. The expression on his face made her stomach flip. 'Have you?'

'No.' Her voice was husky. 'I've only ever slept with—'

'Yes. Same here,' he growled. 'And now you.'

He shut the door behind them, then bent suddenly and kissed her, his mouth sweet and firm. Her fists clenched, then dropped to clutch his shirt. She felt a wash of powerful need and an odd sense of awe as well.

When a man like Byron had had only one woman in his life, it suggested the power and depth of his emotions. To be his second lover *mattered*. It *meant* something. Not just about him, but about herself. She had to deserve this. She had to make it work, however long it lasted. And when it ended, it had to end without bitterness or regret or mess.

The sense of awe and responsibility alchemised to desire, and she held him more tightly, as if he were the only fixed point in a turbulent universe. Their love-making was just as spectacular as it had been the previous Friday night. They stood in the hallway, holding each other around the waist, and kissed softly for a long time. In the silent house, the sounds they made seemed to be magnified. Hayley had never realised that kissing *sounded* so good.

Beyond sound, there was taste and touch, and the touch of his mouth and tongue made her melt inside, and blurred her awareness of everything but Byron and her own body. When he put an arm around her shoulders, held her tightly against him and pulled her towards the bedroom, she went willingly. Then they paused, seated on the edge of the bed, for another timeless interval of tasting each other.

He undressed her slowly today. She was wearing a light cotton cardigan in a frivolous watermelon pink, and he undid its buttons one by one, his fingers brushing the sensitive skin just above her breasts and drifting deliberately to each side as he moved lower down.

She felt heavy and full there, and oddly proud of her tangible response to him. When he peeled the car-

digan off her shoulders, she didn't try to hide what
he'd done to her body, just watched the expectant and
almost reverent way he brought his hands close to
caress her, before sliding her bra straps down and
brushing his knuckles lightly across her exposed nipples.

'Can I do it to you?' she asked huskily, after long,
breathless minutes.

'Please!'

She had never realised before just how much pleasure a woman could get from a line of buttons running
down a man's chest. He wore a soft cotton shirt in a
pattern of cool greyish blues with nothing beneath it.
His chest, as she slowly exposed it to the air, was
even more impressive than she'd remembered.
Strong, naturally tanned, just the right amount of hair.

When she'd finished removing his shirt, she leant
against him, hearing his heartbeat against her ear and
feeling his chest, as solid as the trunk of a well-grown
eucalyptus tree, in her arms. She wanted to spend her
whole life like this.

'Come up a bit higher,' he whispered.

'Why?'

She moved before he'd answered, and then he
didn't need to tell her what he'd meant and what he'd
wanted. His groan of satisfaction said it all. She followed his dark gaze to the place where her breasts
now flattened against his chest and felt a shudder rip-
ple through both of them. It was such an intimate
sight, female against male, skin on skin, yet at some
level she saw it in a blur, already thinking about
the end.

It would have to end. What had he said to her last week in the first aftermath of their love-making?

'An affair. I have to be honest. I can't offer anything else.'

And affairs ended.

All very well to vow that there would be no bitterness or mess, but how did you achieve that?

Perhaps by thinking only about *now*.

Now... Now was good. Very good. She surrendered thought once more.

Byron pulled her down to the bed, taking her weight onto his body, sliding his hands inside the back of her jeans then bringing them round to deftly unfasten the snap at the front. He shimmied them down until she could kick them away, and her slip-on shoes had already disappeared.

'Is it my turn again?' he asked, his breathing uneven.

'*That* was your turn,' she teased, her body's response pulling her more deeply into the moment. 'It's my turn *now*...'

His readiness for her made her task harder. In the end, they both stood and she felt the way he shuddered every time her fingers touched him. When she finally wrapped herself around his naked body, he was hot all over, and his skin was so smooth that all she could do for some minutes was caress him in every place her hands would reach.

They lingered at every new plateau of pleasure, deliberately holding each other back until holding back was no longer possible for either of them. Then it was like the breaking of a dammed and flood-swollen river—powerful, unstoppable, tumultuous and all-consuming.

Afterwards, they both dozed, and he awoke before she did so that when she let her eyes drift open finally she found him watching her, looking thoughtful.

'Tell me,' she ordered, hiding the fluttering of her heart. She wasn't under any illusions. He'd meant what he'd said last week about not wanting love. Maybe she would always be waiting for the axe to fall.

'Wondering how we can organise this in future,' he said.

Practical. Efficient. Organised. Just like she was.

'To find time for it?' she suggested.

'And a place. My mother will probably need to come and live here for a while pretty soon. She'd rather be at her own place, but that's not realistic yet, unless I can think of something that will work. She's…important to me, and I won't give her short shrift.'

Hayley detected the understatement easily.

'Affairs aren't very practical for people like us, are they?'

'No.'

'Do you want to let it go?' she offered, her heart in her mouth.

Don't let him see.

'No.' He didn't hesitate.

'No…'

'Leave it with me, OK?'

'You'll work out a roster?'

'Something like that. If we waited for another night

like last Friday to happen on its own, I think we'd be waiting a long time.'

'Yes, in hindsight, I feel more fond of Tim Foster than I'd ever have thought possible.'

He laughed, and they didn't pick up the issue of how and where they would meet. For the moment, it was too hard to think about.

'She's very reluctant to go into hospital again,' the rehab centre nurse told Byron the following Wednesday. 'She sees it as a backward step.'

'Which of course it is,' he answered.

'Yes, but not a permanent one, in this case. Or it shouldn't be.'

'Mm.' For a moment, Byron couldn't answer properly. His scalp tightened across his temples, warning of a headache to come.

It was ironic that Dad had always seemed the fitter and more able of the two, until prostate cancer had struck him down five years ago. Another irony there. If Dad hadn't felt so confident, so invincible, he might have sought medical advice soon enough to save his life. Mum hadn't really recovered from Dad's death, and when he'd lost Elizabeth a year later, their understanding of what the other was going through had brought them very close.

He thought about the patient Wendy had admitted eleven days ago—the ninety-three-year-old woman with a fractured hip. Pneumonia had followed the fracture, her heart was failing and she'd had several small strokes. She was going downhill rapidly now, and her family had been told that it was only a matter of time. That *wasn't* going to happen to Mum!

'You've got a patient transport vehicle on the way, you said?' he managed to ask the nurse.

'Yes, it should be here any minute.'

'I could have taken her across.'

Going to hospital in an ambulance would only make his mother more aware of the deterioration in her condition. This was just a chest infection, but she wasn't fighting it off the way she should, and a course of oral antibiotics hadn't got rid of it. She would need something stronger, intravenously, as well as a higher level of care than the rehab centre was equipped to provide.

'She's on oxygen, Dr Black,' Sister said patiently. 'She's not managing to maintain her oxygen saturation without it. And she has a drip going in. This bug has also set back her mobility. She really needs the ambulance.'

He would have agreed if it had been any other patient. Had to remind himself that there were people going through this sort of thing all the time. Then he remembered that one of the ambulance drivers could well be Hayley. They'd swapped copies of each other's roster on the weekend in a clandestine, covert little operation disguised as Tori coming over to Max's to play, while the respective mummy and daddy had a cup of tea and a chat.

Byron had been tempted to grab a highlighter pen and block in possible times to see her and to go to bed, but that hadn't felt...right. He'd joked about it to her, and instead was now plotting madly and unproductively in his mind. For several reasons Thursday and Friday were out. So was the weekend.

He couldn't skimp on the time he was giving to his mother at the moment.

He might squeeze in a late visit to Hayley next Tuesday night, but didn't want to promise anything in case it wasn't possible. He was second doctor on call in the department, and if it was a busy night...

Tuesday already seemed like too long to wait, and after that next Wednesday was out. He was as disappointed about it as a child who had dropped a chocolate-coated ice cream after one lick. The sense of distance which had been wrapped around him for so long had simply dissolved, and he felt...*alive* in a way that he'd almost forgotten.

Openly labelling it an affair was good, too. Hayley still had unanswered questions about her ex-husband, while Byron knew the limits of his own heart. So far, it was working.

So, on to the following weekend, which was out, too, unless they just had a picnic with the kids or something. That was likely to lead to frustration more than anything else, since she was part of the on-call crew both nights. Good Lord, how did people manage this when they had to sneak around behind a spouse's back?

Not that this was anything like that. There was no element of sleaziness or deception involved. Still, he felt as if he hadn't got a complete handle on the whole affair thing yet. He also felt what must surely be a very selfish terror that Hayley would decide the game wasn't worth the candle and would politely bail out.

After all, the implication of an affair was that it was a take-it-or-leave-it proposition. No strings attached. No promises made or required. No commitment to riding out the rough spots.

He heard the ambulance pull up at the side of the building and felt an aching urge to see Hayley... which probably meant it wouldn't be her at all, the way life usually worked. As a fully trained paramedic, she'd be the one to get sent to an urgent call ahead of a routine transport job like this.

Hell, it didn't feel routine! This was his mother!

'Hi,' Hayley said softly, as she and Bruce McDonald manoeuvred their stretcher inside.

Byron felt a wash of quite illogical relief at seeing her, for his mother's sake as well as his own. Evidently there were no urgent jobs at the moment.

'She's ready,' he told both Hayley and Bruce, and was disturbed to hear the slight tremble in his voice as his thoughts focused on his mother once more.

Seeing his emotion, she distracted him by teasing him softly, 'Did you get a chance to use that highlighter?' She spoke over her shoulder as she and Bruce wheeled the stretcher with easy familiarity along the corridor.

'Not many places to use it,' he shot back, his feet more firmly on the ground now.

But that didn't last long.

Awareness licked and snaked around both of them, like ribbons of incense smoke. For a moment, he had a flash of how it had first been with Elizabeth so many years ago, but, no, on second thoughts, this was nothing like that. Nothing at all.

He and Elizabeth had felt a quiet certainty about each other from the beginning—a certainty in which physical awareness had been just one thread, equal to all the others. They'd hardly had a day of doubt about each other's feelings. It had all been so very safe and calm, so easy and unruffled.

Arrogant, too, perhaps? On his part, anyway. Back then, he'd been used to getting what he'd wanted. Swimming trophies, good results at school, the offer of a place in Sydney University's highly regarded Faculty of Medicine.

This, by contrast, was a roller-coaster ride, with the dominance of their chemical response to each other sending him to the edge of his seat, making his knuckles metaphorically whiten and his heart jump into his throat. He didn't feel calm at all.

Maybe he just wasn't cut out for something passionate, physical and superficial. Maybe the roller-coaster would leave its rails and throw him into reanimated grief for his lost marriage that would be worse, even, than those first few terrible months of loss.

Dear God! He never wanted to go through that again!

The potential for danger and disaster seemed to have no power at all, however, to discourage the clamouring question inside him, Will it work out for next Tuesday?

'Here we are, Mrs Black,' he heard the rehab nurse say cheerfully in the doorway of his mother's clean, clinical room.

He stepped forward. 'Mum, here are Hayley and Bruce, who found you after your stroke. We're going to get you to hospital, where we'll be able to get rid of this chest bug you've got.'

'Will you come, too, B.J.?' he heard her croak.

Her mouth barely moved, her eyes were closed and

she looked horribly grey and frail. He squeezed her hand between his. Her skin felt loose and thin, as if she'd lost the already minimal layer of fat beneath the skin.

Before he answered her question, he looked up at Hayley and Bruce for confirmation. They nodded.

'Yes, I'll come in the ambulance with you,' he promised.

She opened her dark eyes and smiled, clearly relieved, and he felt a flash of hope. She'd progressed well after the stroke. This was only a chest infection, and she was sixty-eight, not ninety-three. She would be fine, especially if she knew there was a way for her to go home soon.

'Listen,' he said quickly. 'Auntie Valda and Uncle Dean have said they'll come for a few weeks if you want them. I wasn't sure. I know they can get on your nerves, but they mean well.'

'Yes...'

'And if it meant you could be at home sooner...'

'Please!'

'I'll phone them and arrange it. And I spoke to Milly yesterday...' His sister, aged thirty, who was struggling to make it as a fashion designer in London. 'She's going to come out for three weeks in June.'

'Lovely, B.J.! Thank you...' Her grip was weak and crooked in his hand, which felt huge to him suddenly.

Hayley stepped forward. 'Mrs Black, we're going to hook you up to the portable oxygen now, and then we'll be ready to move you to the ambulance. Do you want us to lift you, or could you slide across yourself?'

'I'll slide.'

'That's great.'

'Here.' Bruce grabbed the oxygen equipment.

Byron's mother needed some help in moving, but not as much as he'd feared. She obviously found the simple action tiring, however, and closed her eyes as soon as she was settled. Hayley pulled up an open-weave cotton blanket to keep her warm during the journey, while Bruce took the drip bag off its stand and passed it to the nurse.

Byron had only been in an ambulance once before, years previously, as a medical student. He sat on a fold-down chair behind the driver's seat, leaving Hayley room to manoeuvre beside her patient.

Mum seemed quiescent now, perhaps because he was here, perhaps because of the hope he'd held out about getting her home sooner than planned. It would be much better for all sorts of reasons if she didn't have to come to his place when he was stretched so tight already, dealing with Tori's needs and the demands of his work. Or perhaps Mum was simply quiet because she was feeling too ill to speak.

At the hospital, Hayley and Bruce wheeled her as far as the medical ward and helped her into bed. Byron filled in her admission forms, and a nurse took over her care. She seemed to settle quickly and comfortably.

'We can give you a ride back if your car's there, Byron,' Hayley offered.

He shook his head. 'I'll stay here for a bit, then I'll walk. It's not far, across the playing fields and the park. I've got cover arranged until twelve.'

She hesitated for a moment, glanced at Bruce who

was chatting at a nurse, and to Byron's mother, who was nearly asleep. 'I...uh...found a bit of space on Tuesday night to mark with the highlighter.'

'Mmm, that was my thought, too,' he answered. 'Can't promise.'

'No, I know.'

They shrugged and smiled ruefully, and he suddenly hated the complexity of it, the conflicting pressures and the fact that he had no idea whether in any important sense it would all prove worthwhile. No idea, that was, until she turned to take hold of the stretcher and he felt his groin tighten at the sight of the taut black fabric of her uniform trousers stretched smoothly across her behind.

To hell with important! To hell with this need to keep tabs on his feelings and his fears! For the moment, at least, all he wanted to do was *live* this!

'Made it!'

'Come in.' Hayley drew Byron inside and closed the front door quickly against the autumn evening chill.

He had come straight from the hospital, and he could get called back there at any time. She knew that Robyn had a younger sister who stayed overnight in the spare room at Byron's when he had to work a night shift on call. Apparently that was working well, but Hayley doubted whether it would be an arrangement he'd want to make use of in order to come here regularly on his nights off. He had the same fears as she did about giving his child short shrift.

It was nearly eleven, and she was in her nightgown already, with a heavy satin dressing-gown flung hastily on top. Seductive? Not exactly! In fact, she had been about to give up and go to bed when he'd called a few minutes ago, saying he was free and available now if she wanted him.

Well, she did, of course, although she knew what it would do to her energy levels tomorrow. She had been hoping all evening that if he did make it, it would be reasonably early. Waiting for a man like this felt far too needy. Already she was priming herself to hide the growing depth of her feelings for him.

'How's your mum?' she asked.

'Much, much better. Responding to the new antibiotics, fever down, chest clearing. She should be discharged tomorrow.'

'That's wonderful, Byron! Home?'

'No, another couple of weeks of rehab, unfortunately. But I've talked to my aunt and uncle and they're more than happy to come down. Auntie Valda is sixty-four and very competent. *Too* competent for Mum sometimes, but in this case she'll appreciate it! Hell, what would we do without families? Sorry!' he finished suddenly.

'It's OK. Of course it's all on your mind.'

'I was going on a bit.'

'Is that not permitted or something?' she asked lightly, leading the way to her pretty, casual living room.

'Under the terms of the previously negotiated agreement, you mean?'

'Something like that.'

Byron didn't answer, and for a moment the atmosphere was a little awkward. She didn't want to go straight into his arms with nothing more than a token greeting, as if they had no time to waste on trivial preliminaries. Realistically, however, that was the case.

'Max is asleep?' he asked.

'Hope so, at this hour!'

'Yes...'

'Tea?' She didn't offer wine or beer, knowing he wouldn't drink at this time of night when he was on call.

'Hayley...' he said in a suffering way.

There was a smouldering look of hunger in his eyes, and he must have removed his tie and loosened his collar in the car. Had that been to save time or something? His shirt was open and untidy at the neck, suggesting a rakish impatience for the bedroom.

She thought, Yes, why not? What am I asking for? Why pretend? This is what we agreed it was. And went willingly towards him.

His pager sounded an hour later, not a moment too soon. They both groaned, then laughed.

'Could have been worse,' he said.

'Yes...'

He was dressed and gone within three minutes, and it was somehow impossible just to roll over and go to sleep. She heard his car starting in the drive-way, and had an urgent impulse to watch him leave. Bundled into her dressing-gown with nothing underneath, she raced to the living-room window and was in time to see his red taillights disappear down the street.

'Way it goes,' she said aloud to the silent, deserted street, then turned, went back to bed and read a book she didn't particularly like until a quarter past one. Only then was she relaxed enough to have a chance of sleep.

'Nothing too ambitious,' Byron said.

He crossed his hands smoothly on the steering-wheel to turn out of his street and Hayley couldn't help watching them. She loved his hands, with their lean, adept fingers, the prominent bones at the corner of each wrist, his long forearms, hard and ropy with muscle.

Her stomach gave a little flip of awareness. It was exultant, a little possessive and not remotely safe. She knew she was heading at breakneck speed towards the edge of an emotional precipice, and found it difficult, for a moment, to focus on the pedestrian subject of their picnic with the kids. What did it mean when you called something an affair, yet couldn't imagine that you'd ever want it to end?

'I came equipped for all eventualities,' she said, fighting her need just to go on watching him. 'Beach, nature reserve…'

'I was actually just thinking the playground on the headland above the harbour,' he answered. 'They'll finish eating before we do, and they can play. Afterwards, we could walk down and inspect the fishing boats. Tori always loves that. Maybe pick up some seafood and take it back to my place to cook for dinner.'

'Oh…yes. That sounds so nice!'

And as if he'd really thought about it, too. Chris's plans for a day with Max were always too elaborate for a four-year-old and never worked out. He had been planning a visit this past weekend, but he'd phoned to cancel it on Wednesday night.

'You're right,' he'd said, to end an exchange that had been slightly awkward. 'It's too hard, with all the driving and just one night in between. I'll wait until I can schedule a three-day weekend.'

She had felt left in the lurch at first, so when Byron had proposed this picnic for a rare Monday which they both had off, she'd jumped at it. Max and Tori got on well. To be honest, they were both a bit too strong-willed and exuberant for some of the quieter children at preschool.

'They keep each other busy,' Karen had said recently, in a tone that was a bit stronger than satisfaction but didn't quite convey sheer relief.

Hayley hoped that they would keep each other busy today.

It might only be a picnic table and a rug to laze on at a municipal playground, but they still managed to do it in style. Hayley had brought wine and a Thermos of tea for the adults, and juice and bubbly mineral water for the children, as well as a passion-fruit cake—Mum's recipe—for dessert. Byron produced a tiny Japanese hibachi griller, filled with charcoal briquettes, and proceeded to cook Malay chicken and beef satay sticks with spicy peanut sauce, as well as lamb chops and sausages. He had brought salads and other accompaniments as well.

Tori and Max ate the way grand prix racing cars made pit stops, and hardly seemed to notice that their respective parents were strangely content with merely lazing on a plaid blanket in the dappled shade of some eucalyptus trees.

It was a beautiful day, with an arc of blue sky populated by the occasional cotton-wool cloud and a breeze just strong enough to fluff the waves on the blue-green ocean to tiny white caps. The sound of ropes chinking against aluminum masts carried across the harbour from the marina, and seagulls began to circle and squawk as a fishing boat unloaded its day's catch.

'Will we be able to manage tonight, do you think?' Byron asked, breaking a silence in which a very replete Hayley had almost fallen asleep.

'How do you mean, manage?'

They were lying well apart on the rug, not yet ready to answer questions like, 'Why does Tori's dad have his arms around you, Mummy?' She couldn't help feeling the distance. Given the heat of their contact in bed, it felt unnatural.

'Will the kids think it's strange if you and Max stay overnight?' he asked. 'Will Max say something embarrassing to your parents later on?'

'No, to the first question. I think the kids would be fine about it as long as we answered their questions simply and honestly. Yes, to the second. Max is almost guaranteed to mention it, *and* to phrase it in the most embarrassing way possible!'

She laughed, but Byron didn't.

He was frowning, and murmured, 'Is there any other way we can organise it, I wonder?'

'I don't know.'

She felt uncomfortable that they were discussing it like a problem with a capital P. Watching him, she could see him plotting some alternatives, like a military strategist planning a campaign.

'Would Max be open to staying over with Tori and me on his own?' he finally offered.

'What would be the point of that?'

'You could leave some time during the night—the kids wouldn't know when—and come back and get him the next day, as if it was just a kids' sleep-over party. Then he wouldn't be able to say anything incriminating.'

'But we'd still get our roll in the hay?' she suggested, and despite her best effort to sound casual there was a tart edge to her sweet tone.

There was a beat of silence. 'Yes. We would,' he said. 'Is that not…the goal for you?'

'I think it's possible that I'm a little less goal-oriented than you are on this issue,' she answered him evenly.

'Right. If it's a problem, why haven't you said something?'

Because affairs aren't supposed to get into that sort of territory. Because we haven't promised each other anything. Because if I start asking myself hard questions, I might end up wondering what on earth I'm doing in this situation at all.

She didn't say any of this aloud, just assured him thinly, 'It's not a problem.'

Coward!

She'd been braver about this when they started it, three and a half weeks ago.

She waited for him to challenge her further, but he didn't, and she felt a completely illogical disappointment. There might have been an odd relief in getting backed into a corner and having to say something dramatic and emotional and *defining* about their young relationship. Could you tell the truth more easily in anger or after careful thought?

'We'll forget tonight, then,' he decided for both of them.

'I think I'm…pretty tired, actually. Both nights were busy this weekend, and I didn't get a lot of sleep.'

'Tired? Yes, me, too.'

Which, of course, was the cue for Tori and Max to decide that they needed heavy parental involvement in their play. Since afternoons like this with Max were rarer than Hayley would have liked, she forced some energy back into her body and went to push him on the swing.

He was learning to pump by himself now, but hadn't fully mastered the skill. She coached him strenuously for several minutes. '*Stretch* forward, Max! Now *bend* back. Feel the rhythm, love.'

Then she had to lift him up to the monkey bars and the flying fox. Finally, they were all ready to have an ice cream and a wander around the harbour's three long concrete jetties to look at the boats tied against them. Another commercial fishing boat had just come in, with its swirling beacon of seagulls following overhead.

The boat had a big catch of kingfish to unload into large grey plastic crates, and Max and Tori were both fascinated by the process. Hayley and Byron were kept busy answering their easy questions and asking the crew a couple of harder ones on the children's behalf.

Somehow, by the time four-year-old interest waned, it was already nearly five o'clock.

'Well...' Byron said, as they walked back down the last jetty towards the car park which serviced the harbour and nearby buildings, including the fish shop.

Seafood next. Hayley almost said it, but before she could she saw that Byron had his car keys out and was heading for his vehicle. She went hot. Hadn't they planned to...?

Not any more, apparently.

If they hadn't had those moments of coolness earlier, she might have reminded him about it, but she didn't want to now. She doubted that he had forgotten. He just wasn't interested any more, since cooking and eating together would no longer be a precursor to a session in bed.

She was shocked at how disappointed she was, and how much it *hurt*. This wasn't supposed to hurt. It wasn't supposed to end with her feeling used and slighted by a man she'd always thought of as considerate of the feelings of others.

She glanced sideways at him, realised they hadn't exchanged a word to each other since getting up from the picnic rug. Or, at least, not a word that hadn't been filtered through the children and intended for public consumption.

Was he angry?

She risked another sideways glance as they each slipped a child into one of the two booster seats in the back of his spacious late-model blue car, but couldn't decipher the meaning of his expression. Disappointed, certainly. Beyond that...

Her heart sank. He was the one who'd answered, 'We'll forget tonight.' But perhaps he blamed her for it, all the same.

Several minutes later, when they reached her place and parted with the sorts of politeness and thanks Hayley was strict about with Max, she was still unhappy and confused, and nothing in Byron's manner, as he said goodbye, gave her a reason not to be.

CHAPTER SEVEN

BY THE time Max was asleep in bed that night, Hayley had had enough. She phoned an old friend, a desperate measure which she resorted to only in the most extreme circumstances.

'Could you come over and sit with Max for a while?' she asked Melanie. 'He's asleep, but I need to get out for a bit.'

'Sure, Hayl. Just suffering from overload?'

'Something like that,' she agreed carefully.

'I don't know how you do it, I really don't.'

'You've got three kids.'

'Yeah, but I've got a pretty good husband, too! I'll be over in about half an hour, OK?'

Melanie arrived in twenty minutes, with something that was probably pizza dough dried on the front of her sweatshirt and her hair a cheerful brown mess. She didn't ask any awkward questions, just pushed Hayley out the door and said, 'Don't come back until you feel better, OK?'

'Well, that could be a few days!'

'Bad girl!' Melanie laughed.

Five minutes later, Hayley met Byron's surprised... then pleased...face at his front door.

'Hey...!' He drew her in, grinning. 'Tori's not quite asleep yet. We'd better wait until she is before we start—'

'No,' she said. The new, uplifted mood his face

had produced in her shut off like a light. 'This isn't good enough, Byron.'

There was a flash of surprise and shock in the depths of his golden brown eyes.

'No, I can see that,' he said, watching her guardedly.

'You know, we could have had a lovely evening, pottering around the kitchen together, drinking a glass of wine. We could have made garlic prawns or something, and had music playing, and— But no. There was no prospect of bed at the end of it, so you weren't interested. Maybe I'm changing the terms, or something, but— No! I never thought that an affair meant nothing *but* sex!'

Byron looked harassed, which was probably understandable, given her tone and the fact that she'd only just made it inside the front hall before commencing her verbal assault.

'Come through to the kitchen,' he said. 'I'm still washing up. If Tori thinks something interesting is happening, though, she'll be up out of bed like a Jack-in-the-box. We should talk quietly.'

Which she hadn't been, of course. Her voice had been out of control.

She took a deep breath. 'OK. Sorry.'

'Tea? Wine?' He'd already turned back to stack his dishwasher.

'I'm fine, thanks.'

That earned a sharp glance which said, I get it. You've planned a short stay. Fair enough.

'I told you before this even started that I couldn't promise you anything, Hayley,' he said aloud. He grabbed a large frying-pan from the sink, and Hayley saw the remnants of scrambled egg sticking to the sides. His and Tori's evening meal.

'I know,' she answered him. 'I'm not asking for promises, am I?'

'But you'd like more than just sex?' The frying-pan made a clatter as he slotted it into the dishwasher.

'Too blunt, Byron.'

'OK, you don't want it blunt. When we talk about it *or* when we do it. You want the trimmings.'

'I think so. Some of them.'

'Which ones?'

'I don't know! You're not making this easy!'

'I wanted to bring you and Max back for seafood this afternoon,' he said quietly, turning to face her. 'But after our earlier discussion, I assumed you'd rather not. I really wasn't thinking that if there was no…uh…prospect of a goal, as you phrased it, then there was no point in playing the game at all. Please, don't think that.'

'We obviously didn't communicate particularly well today,' she agreed, in an attempt to meet him halfway.

'Are we doing better now?'

'Mmm, possibly. I guess I do want the odd *trimming* here and there.'

'I'll see what I can do.'

They smiled at each other uncertainly, both of them knowing that something wasn't right.

'Shall I help you with this?' she said, gesturing at the picnic things he still hadn't stacked into the dishwasher.

'It's fine. Have you got a neighbour sitting with Max, or something?'

'A friend.' She could see his inner debate like the workings on a transparent clock. Might she stay for a while after all? Helping him out—the answer was still no, but perhaps her stubbornness wasn't good for either of them—she added, 'So I should get back. She has three kids of her own, so I only ask her in an emergency.'

'This was an emergency?'

She flushed. 'I was steaming a bit, yes.'

'Angry with me?'

'Yes.'

'Ah.' He controlled a sigh, as if he found her a nuisance suddenly, and she left a short while later, feeling hot and awkward and as if her emotional visit had only made things worse, pushing them farther apart instead of clearing the air.

'We've got some drama,' Bruce reported as soon as he'd finished taking the emergency call. 'Need both crews, Priority One. Two fishermen off the rocks.'

'Who else are they calling in?' trainee ambulance officer Lucas Garrett asked.

Newly qualified paramedic Alison Carmichael, standing by the sink, put down the coffee-mug into which she'd just spooned some granules of instant coffee.

'SouthCare chopper, for the moment,' Bruce answered. 'But they've alerted the State Emergency Service and the hospital.'

'Are they still in the water?'

'Yes, but it's the classic problem. They both tried to get back out where they fell in and got smashed against the rocks by another wave. We've got their mate reporting on his mobile, and he must have only just been in range because it's not an easy spot to get to. Let's go, guys. Who knows what we'll find by the time we get there?'

'Where is it, Bruce?' Hayley asked.

'Wouldn't you know it? It's Robson's Point.'

'I guess the fishing must be pretty good there,' Alison said, 'because this is the third time I've heard about problems at Robson's Point since I started here.'

'Yeah, and do you know why the fishing's so good?' Lucas came in. 'They feed off the blood of the mugs that get washed in!'

'Save it for the pub, Lucas,' Hayley told him.

He was prone to macabre humour as his way of dealing with some of the things they had to see in this job. It wasn't Hayley's style, but she understood where the need came from.

Paired with Lucas today, and much more experienced than he was, she let him take the wheel and began to write up the call-out report as they drove. Robson's Point was about ten kilometres south on the highway. As Lucas had suggested, it was a popular fishing spot, but it was accessible only by a rough four-wheel-drive track that meandered for a good two kilometres through the bush.

Just south of the point was a beautiful but treacherous stretch of beach, known for its rips and currents, and the point itself consisted of a horizontal shelf of rock that tempted fishermen too close to its edge in search of the fish that shoaled beneath its sheltering overhang.

Above this shelf was a near-vertical cliff face of

broken rock, and the point had two jagged prongs which curved around an extension of the rock shelf that was almost impossible to reach except at low tide. Despite warning signs posted beside the make-shift car park at the end of the track, surfers, hikers, swimmers and fishermen had got into trouble at this spot many times.

Before they'd even turned off the highway, dis-patcher Kathy Lowe came back on the radio with an update.

'SouthCare helicopter's on its way, with two aero-med qualified paramedics on board, but we've got a complication,' she told both ambulance crews. 'One of the fishermen got knocked unconscious on the rocks, and the mate has jumped in after him. I've got a bystander on another mobile saying the second fish-erman has washed up onto the shelf at the bottom of the cliff with what looks like a broken leg. He's on the very edge of signal range and keeps getting cut off, so I'm not getting much clear detail. I've called in the State Emergency Service as well, just in case, because I know Robson's Point…'

'Yeah, we all do,' Lucas muttered.

'And I can't see you guys getting to him without help with the winching equipment.'

'Copy that, Kathy,' Hayley said. 'Sounds like it's going to be quite a party.'

Lucas swore as he took the heavy vehicle over the ruts and gutters in the track, and they tipped and lurched dramatically from side to side. It was a four-wheel-drive ambulance especially suited for rural and off-road conditions, but that didn't make the track it-self any smoother.

'We're not going to want to take fractures out this way, are we?' he said.

'Wouldn't be fun for them,' Hayley agreed. 'And if there's the possibility of spinal injuries…' She shook her head. 'Let's see if Kathy can get us a second chopper.'

She contacted the dispatcher again, but Kathy had to report a few minutes later, 'There may be a problem with it. Careflight is off-line for maintenance. I'm trying Westpac.'

Finally, they glimpsed the beach. A wash of dark blue water and pale sand beyond scrubby, yellow-flowered bushes, it looked alluring and beautiful beneath the mild autumn sunshine. Just ahead of them was the roughly cleared section of scrub that served as a car park, currently occupied by five vehicles, three of them four-wheel-drive.

'Wish I could get closer,' Lucas muttered. 'Hang on. If I back up and take the creek-bed for a bit, there's a way.' His inexperience was showing a little.

'Don't get bogged down,' Hayley warned. 'This must turn to sand pretty soon.'

'This vehicle should be fine. How do you fancy carrying an eighty-kilo stretcher case for two hundred metres, though?'

'If we have to.'

Bruce seemed to have made the same decision as Hayley—better a longer trek than the risk of getting the vehicle stuck. The car he was driving wasn't designed for off-road conditions. He parked in the car park, then he and Alison grabbed some gear and followed Car Eleven on foot.

Lucas covered an extra thirty metres before he was

forced to concede defeat, even with four-wheel-drive
and high clearance. He made a nine-point turn so that
he'd be able to drive straight out once they had a
patient on board, and parked beside what could be a
good landing spot for a helicopter, if that was necessary.

They heard another vehicle, and a State Emergency
Service truck ploughed around the end of the car park
and powered past them.

Was that Byron?

Hayley had caught a glimpse of a familiar silhouette in the front passenger seat, but didn't quite believe it—not until he emerged from the vehicle, which
had managed to get a little farther, almost to the start
of the beach, just below the cliff face. He was a lone
non-uniformed figure amidst several SES volunteers
in their bulky orange uniforms.

'You guys made pretty good time on that track,'
Lucas told the SES team leader. He sounded a little
grudging about it.

'Lighter vehicle, that's all,' the other man returned.

'Byron?' Hayley asked. He looked well prepared
for the likely conditions, in heavy hiker's boots, casual grey trousers, a flannel shirt and a light jacket.

All the same, her tone conveyed, Why are you
here? She felt awkward with him, since she hadn't
expected to see him. Their last parting hadn't been
nearly as positive as she'd have liked. She sensed that
there was a crisis point building in their affair. Wondered why she'd ever thought that any kind of relationship, no matter what you called it, could be simple
with a man like Byron.

'Thought I might be of more use here than waiting

at the hospital, since things are quiet there this morning,' he answered her. His brown eyes flashed briefly into hers, glinting with gold. He didn't look comfortable either.

'Cutting out the middle man, eh?' Bruce said. His humour cut across their unwilling eye contact and eased the tension.

With more than one service included now—ambulance professionals, hospital-based doctor and emergency service volunteers—there was no obvious chain of command. Much therefore depended on the goodwill of those involved, and their tacit agreement to put efficiency ahead of territoriality. Sadly, there had been incidents in the past, in other parts of the state, where that hadn't happened.

They all moved quickly to the best and safest vantage point, an upthrusting outcrop of rock near the seaward edge of the rock shelf. Hayley could see how deceptive the waves were beneath the blue sky. The swell was long, and there were intervals of quieter waves before a series of four or five suddenly broke much harder and higher.

Out beyond the breaking point, in a part of the ocean that was dark with unanchored patches of tan-colored weed, two of the three fishermen bobbed like tiny, lonely corks.

A closer look showed that one of them was supporting the other in a trained and appropriate lifesaving hold. Correctly, the stronger man was making no attempt to swim closer to the rocks and, in fact, it soon became apparent that the ocean's currents were slowly pulling the pair further out.

'He's doing the right thing, as long as he doesn't panic or tire,' Bruce said.

'Any idea how long until the helicopter gets here?' the SES team leader asked.

'About ten minutes, based on our best information,' Bruce answered. 'Unfortunately we've just heard that the Westpac chopper is out on a routine retrieval.'

'SouthCare can carry two patients, as long as only one of them is serious.'

'We've got a surf lifesaving boat on its way down from Arden Beach, but it has to hug the coast so it's not fast,' said Bruce. 'I doubt it'll arrive in time to be of much use.'

'Meanwhile, we need to focus on the third bloke at the bottom of the cliff,' said a second SES volunteer. 'I wish we could see him from here because we've got an incoming tide, and I know this point better than I'd like.'

'So do I,' Bruce agreed grimly.

'We'll have to go down the cliff for him.'

'Where's the guy who called in on the second mobile?'

'Lost contact.'

'Pity. I'd like more detail on that as well. I thought he'd be waiting for us down here.'

Byron didn't wait to hear any more, and let the various voices blend together. He left the rocks and began to push his way up through the tangled scrub on the headland to reach a vantage point at the top of the cliff, knowing some of the others would soon follow.

His instinct told him that this was one of those emergencies that could still go either way. If the chopper lifted the two water-bound fishermen to safety with no problems, and if the third man at the bottom of the cliff could be reached and moved easily, they might all be on their way out of here within twenty minutes and his presence wouldn't have been necessary at all.

If neither of those things happened that smoothly, however, his decision to join the team could make a crucial difference.

His thighs worked as he pushed his way towards the top of the cliff, his breathing was deep and he held his forearms in front of his face to ward off the scratchy branches of the bushes which threatened to whip against him.

Professionally, he was anxious about what he'd find, alert to the possibility of serious injury and major headaches in getting the injured men to safety. Personally, the vertigo that dizzied him had nothing to do with his rising height on the headland, above jagged rocks and powerful waves, and everything to do with Hayley's anger over the weekend. His response to what she was giving out was so complicated and confused. A part of him wanted to drop the whole thing as soon as he decently could. Get back to the familiar ache of loneliness and loss, rather than this new yet scarcely more comfortable sense that Hayley wasn't happy and it was his responsibility to do something about it.

Because if he didn't do something about it, she'd go back to Chris. That had been her starting point after all. That this affair would help her to find out how she felt about Chris.

I don't want her to go back to Chris!

He felt a sweat breaking out on the back of his neck and his upper lip which was only partly due to physical effort.

I don't want her to, and that means I'm getting in too deep. I have to keep it cool, distant. The way it would have been with Wendy. An affair, like Hayley and I agreed on. I don't want to end it, but I need to pull back. How?

'Hell, as if I have time to think about this now!' he muttered aloud, and turned back for a moment and watched the others. Bruce McDonald and his shift partner were climbing the headland behind him, along with two State Emergency Service volunteers. Two more volunteers were checking the lower route around the rocks. One of them was using his radio, while Hayley and Lucas were waiting at their vehicle.

Byron heard the SouthCare chopper in the distance, approaching rapidly. If the two fishermen could be winched from the ocean by the specially trained aero-med paramedics aboard the aircraft, it could then off-load the uninjured patient by landing on a smooth piece of grassy ground near Hayley's vehicle before flying the unconscious man directly to Canberra.

The stronger fisherman had now been in the water supporting his injured friend for almost half an hour and would be getting very cold and tired. Hayley and Lucas would need to assess him for hypothermia and superficial injuries such as lacerations from the rocks. Byron's own expertise was more likely to be needed with the third fisherman—the one who should come into sight once he'd climbed another ten metres up this headland.

Byron breasted the top of the headland and felt the

sudden onrush of a strong breeze from the ocean. For a moment, he was arrested by the sight of the helicopter wheeling around at what seemed an impossibly steep angle as its pilot, doctor and paramedics assessed the scene below.

He was about to turn his attention to the rock shelf where, according to the report they'd received, the third fisherman should be lying. But then his eye was caught by a moving shape in the water, between the rocks and the two fishermen.

What kind of fish moved like that? Or was it a lone dolphin?

No, Lord, no! It was a shark.

CHAPTER EIGHT

A SHARK, right there in the water below the rock shelf.

There was absolutely nothing that Byron could do except sweat and pray and watch. The pale shape was nosing around the shelf that was pincered by the two cliffs jutting out from this headland. A fin broke the water briefly, and any doubt he'd still had about the creature disappeared. It was definitely a shark. A large one, probably a white pointer.

Why was it so attracted to this section of rock? It was swimming in a kind of figure eight, a movement pattern that was elegant and primitively efficient. His focus shifting to the rocks themselves, Byron saw the injured fisherman now, but he was lying ominously still against a rough, slightly harder outcrop of stone.

Blood in the water? That had to be what was attracting the shark, but the creature wasn't like a crocodile. It couldn't lunge up onto the rocks to seize the prey it could sense there. The man was in no immediate danger.

A wave broke over the shelf, dissipating in pretty, fan-shaped patterns of white which reached the injured man as harmless ruffles only about a centimetre deep. But the tide was coming in, Byron remembered. Was the man safely beyond the rising water's reach?

He heard a faint cry and had a momentary wash of huge relief.

He's conscious. I can call to him. If he could only crawl a few metres more across that shelf...

But then he realised that it wasn't the injured fisherman who was calling but someone else, a man, much closer at hand.

'Help me! Is anybody there?'

Hell, who was this? Did they have a fourth casualty involved?

Two of the SES volunteers reached Byron at that moment. They were both well-built middle-aged men, and had a radio.

'I think we've located the man who called in on the second mobile,' Byron yelled back to them as he edged towards the cliff face.

'Is there a problem?'

'I'm about to find out. Hey, down there!' he shouted. 'Can you hear me?'

'I've hurt my leg.' The male voice was panicky. 'I was trying to get down to the one on the rocks, but I fell.'

Byron lowered himself to his stomach, hearing the SES radio crackling and blaring in the background as one of the two volunteers relayed the news to his team leader and began to list the likely equipment they would need. From this position, he could just see the man, lying on his side and clinging precariously to a rough lip of rock about halfway down the twenty-metre-high cliff.

Lifting his gaze, he saw the chopper sitting in a hover over the two men in the water. They had begun to lower a paramedic, a black shape dressed in wet-suit, face mask, snorkel and flippers, and harnessed to the end of a winch line.

OK, so one man on the cliff, one on the rocks and two in the water. But where was the shark?

Byron looked for the pale shape, but it was no longer in its holding pattern near the rocks. Had it gone? Found a more rewarding hunting ground further along? He couldn't see it anywhere, and couldn't spend the time to keep looking. That didn't mean he was in any danger of forgetting it was out there somewhere…

'We've got help on the way,' he called down to the man on the cliff. 'Can you tell me your name?'

'Colin. Colin Frederick.'

'Colin, I'm a doctor, and we've got SES and paramedics, ropes and harnesses and stretchers and a ton of other stuff, as well as that chopper out there. We're going to get you up safely as soon as we can.'

'Yeah, I called in about the guys in the water.'

'That helped a lot, Colin, otherwise we wouldn't have known that the third one had gone in after his mate.'

'Stupid to try this cliff on my own. I did it once as a kid, but I'm not as agile now. The guy hasn't moved, and that tide's coming in.'

'It's all right. We've got crew handling that.'

'He was moving at first. He got himself up out of the water, but he looked pretty bad. I'm OK. I mean, I'm holding on. The other guy, when he stopped moving, that was when I decided—'

'Don't tire yourself out, OK, Colin? I just want to check out a couple of things.'

He ran through a quick checklist of routine questions. The injured man seemed to be oriented in time and space. He knew his name and the date, and could answer a simple question on current affairs. There was some bleeding apparently, but not enough to frighten him. And, of course, there was pain.

Meanwhile, two figures were slowly rising out of the sea towards the chopper as the winch turned. The man who was left in the water, the one who'd held his unconscious mate afloat for more than half an hour now, looked hardly bigger than a matchstick out there, and very, very alone.

The shark, Byron kept thinking. Where's the shark?

The question was like a knot pulling tighter and tighter in his stomach. In a calculated decision, he didn't dare tell anyone else about it in case it spread the panic he was fighting to suppress in himself. That chopper crew was already working as fast as it could with safety. Knowing about the shark wouldn't speed them up.

Less logically but just as powerfully, if he talked about the shark, the danger would become more solid and real.

He scanned the water but still couldn't see it. Saw instead another large wave breaking over the rocks. Those waves were beautiful but treacherous today, each one of them powerful muscles of cold, glass-green water. This time the wave reached the injured man with greater force and covered his legs to a depth of ten or twelve centimetres before it ebbed. Once more, it would have washed the smell of his blood back into the water.

The chopper still hovered, the beat of its blades dry and fast. They must be detaching the harness by now and making their first assessment of their patient's injuries and depth of unconsciousness. The SES volunteers were still co-ordinating their plans over the radio. No sign of the surf lifesaving boat yet, and in any case it couldn't beach safely anywhere near those rocks. Once the chopper had the second fisherman safely out of the water, the boat would undoubtedly be sent back to base.

'The tidal shelf is a no-go,' Byron heard indistinctly over the radio. 'Tide's too high already, and the swell is getting heavier.'

Feeling the wind up here, Byron wasn't surprised at this decision.

'So we'll go down from up here?' the SES man radioed back.

'That's right, mate,' came the answer. 'Can you start checking out how we're going to lash the ropes?'

'We're already on it.'

'Sounds good,' Byron commented, and relayed the news down to Colin, knowing how important it was to keep the injured man informed, optimistic and a part of what was going on.

He watched the winch line going down to the water again, the black figure at the end of it so tiny against the vast backdrop of the sea. Byron began to relax a little. One casualty safe, a second one almost there.

Almost… But then he caught sight of the shark once more. It was no longer nosing around the rocks. It had found an easier meal already in the water. Once again, he went cold. Must have let a sound escape from his lips because one of the volunteers looked at him with raised eyebrows.

'Thorn,' he said in explanation, then snapped his mouth shut so hard that his teeth jarred.

Dear God, if no one else had seen it, he wasn't

going to tell them! Especially not now. He held his breath, every muscle aching with tension as he watched the shape in the water, lost it amongst the weeds, saw it again, closer to the point where the harness was still dropping steadily from the chopper. The paramedic had plunged into the ocean now.

He heard the blood pounding in his head and kept thinking There had to be something he could do, although he knew there wasn't. Scare it off? How? Warn the chopper pilot? To achieve what?

The shark veered off course, distracted by something, and he began to breathe again. The SES radio crackled out a report relayed from the chopper pilot about the first casualty. The initial assessment from the paramedic on board wasn't good, and the patient needed high level treatment. They'd drop the other man on the ground if his condition was good enough and head straight for Canberra.

There was some difficulty with getting the fisherman into the harness. He had to be tired. Or was he panicking and fighting the paramedic's experienced actions? Byron saw the shark, well away from the fisherman, circling around. Was the creature spooked by the chopper somehow? He didn't know enough, not nearly enough, about the behaviour of sharks.

No, it wasn't spooked. It was coming back, faster than he'd yet seen it move, and it was heading straight for the man who was still struggling with the harness.

Byron felt a sickening surge of bile in his gut. There was no doubt now about the shark's intent. Oh, dear God, get that harness on! Get it *on*! Yes! Yes...

But before the harness was fully secure, the helicopter suddenly lurched a metre or more out of its steady hover and almost seemed to leap upward. The two men's legs cleared the water when the shape of the shark was about three metres off. It lunged from the water suddenly, and he got a glimpse of a dark, gaping maw. Above the waves, the two men still weren't properly positioned, and dangled precariously.

Don't let them fall! The winch line was rising fast. That had to be close to its maximum speed of forty-five metres a minute.

The shark had circled away, already programmed for its next quest, but if the fisherman and the paramedic fell... Byron saw the paramedic's body stiffen as if he was yelling, but the sound of chopper blades and ocean waves drowned a mere human voice. The winch wound rapidly upwards, and they both hung on, just. Finally, they reached the chopper's skid and were soon pulled to safety. The chopper continued further out to sea then around in a wide, slow arc towards the sandy beach.

Thank God it was over.

With legs like melted rubber, Byron stood up and said to the SES volunteers, 'I'm heading down in case I'm needed with the chopper. I'll be back up here by the time you're ready to send someone down the cliff.' He called down to Colin, in a voice that still sounded rusty and unsteady to his own ears, 'I'm going to leave you with the guys here, Colin. They'll look after you while their team gets the ropes set up.'

At first, his legs threatened to go on strike and his descent from the headland was like a poorly controlled fall more than anything else. Another second and they'd all have seen a sickening boil of blood and movement in the water. But someone in the chopper must have seen that moving shape as Byron had, just in time. They hadn't been able to warn the cold, clinging fisherman or the paramedic who'd gone to bring him up, and they'd almost lost both of them. If the men hadn't succeeded in clinging on...

Byron's descent to the ambulance was much quicker than the climb up, and he arrived just as the chopper touched down. Hayley and Lucas were waiting in the back of the vehicle. The chopper paramedics offloaded the less seriously injured fisherman on a light, portable stretcher and brought him to the ambulance. All three men looked white and tense, and Byron saw Hayley frown and exchange a glance with Lucas.

Then she registered Byron's face, too, and he knew he looked as shaken as the others did.

'What happened?' she asked.

Byron shook his head. 'Tell you later.'

'Hairy out there?' Lucas asked.

'Later,' Byron repeated, on a growl this time.

Alison arrived, a little breathless. 'Bruce wants me to sit in the back with this one, Hayley,' she said, 'in case they need you here.'

'This one's in pretty good shape,' Hayley agreed. 'Some lacerations from the rocks, early hypothermia. Fully conscious. Basically, he's just exhausted after being in the water and supporting his friend for so long.'

'He should be admitted overnight for observation,' Byron said.

'We'll let them know that's what you wanted, if

there's any talk of sending him home,' Hayley answered. 'Who's on today?'

'Can't remember.' He dropped his voice, since Alison and Lucas were both in the back of the vehicle with the patient now and no one else was listening at the moment, and added, 'Yours is the only roster I've memorised.'

He wasn't quite sure why he'd chosen this moment to try and restore a connection that he'd contemplated ending just a short while ago.

The humour didn't deflect her—hardly surprising—and she touched his arm, the caring in her face very real and clear.

'Seriously, Byron, you look so shaken up. If there's something else going on, don't I need to hear?'

But he only shook his head, didn't want to admit yet that the possibility of a shark attack was still real. Every wave that reached the third fisherman, still apparently unconscious, washed more of his blood into the water, and as the tide rose, the likelihood of him getting washed back into the sea grew stronger.

If it happens, let him stay unconscious, Byron found himself thinking. Let him not be aware...

He noted the distance and disappointment in Hayley's expression, but didn't have time to deal with it now. Would it be better if the awkwardness remained and things just drifted to a finish? Alison and Lucas were ready to leave, and the SES crew on the cliff top, now joined by the rest of the team, as well as Hayley, Bruce and himself, would soon have their ropes and harnesses ready.

Byron didn't talk about what he'd seen until they were all gathered on the cliff top and ready to make the descent. 'Speed is a real priority,' he said, cutting across the SES team leader's outline of the plan. 'I saw a shark circling those rocks earlier.'

He didn't want it to be a melodramatic announcement, but inevitably it was, even though he avoided any description of the fisherman's paper-thin avoidance of death.

'Is that why you were so white?' Hayley asked, under cover of the renewed flurry of activity.

'I'll tell you later,' he told her again.

She gave him a silent, wide-eyed look, then shrugged.

He thought, Damn! As if we could just 'drift'! Whatever happens, it's going to involve some kind of explosion, and pieces to pick up afterwards.

The SES crew had rigged up three sets of ropes, one attached to the sturdy base of a tree and the other two to a protruding piece of solid rock. One rope would be used only for the lowering of equipment.

Two men were already on their way down, and Byron told them, 'Check for any possible spinal injury. Hold off on moving him unless there seems to be no choice. Hayley and I will get a spinal board and a neck brace onto him as soon as we get down.'

Colin had already been told he would have to wait a little longer.

The two volunteers, both experienced climbers, reached the bottom of the cliff in good time, released their harnesses and signalled that the ropes could be safely pulled up. Two more SES people then helped Byron and Hayley into the harnesses and instructed them on the safe way to tackle the descent. Meanwhile, Bruce and the remaining orange-suited volunteer lowered a Stokes stretcher filled with equipment on the third rope.

The middle-aged fisherman didn't show any evidence of spinal or head injury. Possibly he was simply suffering from hypothermia, but Byron and Hayley worked quickly to attach the spinal board and neck brace to play it safe. Basal skull fractures were difficult to detect in field conditions. The man's blood pressure and pulse weren't brilliant either.

'There could be an internal injury,' Hayley said. 'Should we stabilise here?'

The decision would have been hers without Byron's presence, and she had no real need to defer to him. The SES crew had no desire to weigh in with an opinion, and made it clear in the way they were standing back.

'I'd rather get him off the ground,' Byron said. 'He's been here a while.'

'I can handle these conditions, if that's what you're worried about.'

'You can handle conditions that would give me nightmares, with your experience,' Byron answered bluntly. 'That's not the issue.'

'Let's do it, then,' she agreed.

The man's right leg was obviously seriously broken. He must have only just managed to haul himself to relative safety. After two SES men had carried the patient beyond the reach of the incoming tide, Byron quickly splinted the leg, with Hayley's assistance.

Laying him on a blanket in the Stokes stretcher and placing a second blanket on top, the SES men strapped him in, shielding his face with their hands to prevent an accidental lashing from the wayward

ends of the straps. Taking a neck pulse once again—
it was holding steady—Byron smelled the synthetic
odour of the new-looking straps for a moment above
the stronger salt smell of the sea.

'Prepare to lift… And lift.' All four of them were
needed for the task of moving patient and stretcher to
the base of the cliff, and after the next instruction of,
'Prepare to lower…and lower,' came, Byron had to
stretch the stiffness out of his hand. Definitely a good
eighty kilos. He began to calculate the dose of morphine he would use once they reached the ambulance,
if the man's blood pressure was high enough.

The SES team leader came up to him. 'I saw the
shark while you were putting on that neck brace,' he
said quietly. 'Big fella, wasn't he? A pointer.'

'Circling at the edge of the shelf?'

'Yep. With the way those waves were building,
fifteen minutes later and we'd have been too late.'

'He's not in great shape as it is. How are we going
with getting him up the cliff?'

'They've got a pulley rigged at the top, above the
spot just here where it overhangs. The way we'll rig
it, it'll keep him pretty level. We can get him to the
ambulance for you, then it's over to you.'

'We need an update on the Westpac chopper,'
Byron answered. 'I'd hate you to have to take him
out on that track, Hayley.'

'I know,' she answered. 'I was thinking that as we
came in, before I knew what we'd be looking at here.'

'We're ready to go.'

There was a shout from the top of the cliff. 'Update
on the Westpac chopper. Another forty minutes.'

'Ten would have been about right,' Byron said.

Hayley nodded. 'We can keep working on him in the back of the car, though.'

In fact, it took them nearly twenty minutes to get the patient back to the ambulance. He remained unconscious, but moaned several times and muttered some incomprehensible words.

Inside the vehicle, Byron told Hayley, 'Can you start a drip, check his obs and run in some morphine, if he'll tolerate it, while I check him for internal injuries?' She was already setting up oxygen equipment.

'There's going to be something,' she predicted. 'Blood pressure's dropped further.'

'We've got the MAST suit.'

'I'll set it up.'

Byron palpated each quadrant of the man's abdomen, earning another moan from the patient when he tested the upper left side. With the tell-tale rapid, thready pulse and dropping blood pressure, it could mean a lacerated spleen, and he wished he knew how many times the fisherman had been thrown against the rocks.

The MAST suit was an obvious precaution, but the morphine was a judgement call. Narcotics always depressed respiration. What if he and Hayley were wrong about the absence of head injuries, and the drug he was giving acted to further suppress an already compromised central nervous system? On the other hand, severe pain was debilitating in itself and this man couldn't afford anything more that sapped his strength.

'At least the shark is out of the frame!' Byron muttered.

Hearing the words, Hayley looked across at him. He still seemed tense, and she wondered what he wasn't saying. She almost pushed him about it again, then decided against it.

It was good to be working so closely beside him like this, and their thinking was similar in these emergency conditions. She was glad he'd decided against further stabilising the patient on-site. Why risk the tentative harmony, out of curiosity or this need—she couldn't get rid of it—to feel uniquely close to him? They were much closer to each other like this, working well together, than they would be if she nagged at him to download whatever had happened earlier. He hadn't sought much in the way of special connection today.

Meanwhile, using a second Stokes stretcher, the SES volunteers had reached Colin Frederick and were preparing to bring him up. A radio report from the cliff top suggested that the man's injuries were relatively minor—a broken lower leg, twisted ankle and some fairly dramatic cuts and grazes, but nothing of a life-threatening nature. Another piece of good luck. If he hadn't managed to cling to that ledge on the way down...

Hayley shuddered. She and Byron were temporarily alone with this patient and there was nothing to do now but keep checking his vital signs and await the chopper. They had oxygen and Haemaccel going in, a slower and stronger pulse and better blood pressure. After all the drama of the day, it was oddly peaceful, and she desperately wanted to say something to her lover to seal the moment.

I'm sorry about overreacting the other day. You didn't deserve it. Can we backtrack a bit?

You look gorgeous in blue-grey, with the wind combing your hair.

If I kiss you, will you get some colour back into your face and stop looking like you've seen a ghost?

'That shark…' he said at last, before Hayley could find the right words. 'I saw it before the chopper even arrived. It was so close to getting that second guy in the water, I could almost smell the blood. Another second, Hayley…'

He sketched the details, his words jerky and vivid in the pictures they conjured up. He finished with a helpless shake of his head, 'There wasn't a thing I could do, and I could only think that if I let everyone know, it would just make it worse. *All* of us watching with our hearts in our mouths, seeing him die that way? That chopper crew couldn't have worked any faster. I had to bottle it inside… Hated feeling that helpless. Sorry I'm unloading it all onto you now.'

'I wanted you to,' she answered him quickly. 'I knew there was something.'

'About the other night…'

'I'm sorry. It was a huge over-reaction on my part.'

'No, it wasn't. You were right.' He snapped his mouth shut again, as if he'd said everything that needed saying.

'Let's…' she began. 'I mean, could we—?'

'Let's not say a whole lot of stuff,' he cut in, hardly moving his mouth. It looked tight and numb. 'I'm thinking about a few things. Please, don't—' He broke off.

After a few seconds, she said carefully, 'Don't crowd you?'

'Something like that.'

'Fair enough.' Could he hear the lump in her throat that was straining her voice? Apparently not.

'I'll have Robyn's sister stay with Tori after she's asleep one night next week and come over to you and we'll see how it works out.'

'That'll be great.' Oh, what an effort! She had a horrible sense that this was the beginning of the end.

'Hey, is there anything we can do? Has there been an accident?' Two curious fishermen, rods and buckets in hand, came around to the back of the ambulance at that moment and stood at a respectful distance.

'There's another one on the way,' Byron answered. The men whistled, and he added, 'Do you ever fish off Robson's Point?'

'No, we park here then walk down to the next headland,' answered the older man. 'It's a trek, but it's safer. A couple of guys got washed off, did they?'

'That's right.'

They whistled again. 'Saw a shark down our way and wondered if it could have been that. You sure there's nothing we can do?'

'All under control, thanks,' Hayley said. She heard the air start to beat in the distance. They could all hear it now—the sound of helicopter blades chopping up the sky.

'We'll leave you to it, then,' the younger of the two fishermen concluded, and they walked towards their car.

'It's been a long morning,' Byron said.

'Almost there.' Hayley smiled at him, and they sat

hand in hand for a few precious moments as they watched the helicopter and the remainder of the rescue crew, with Colin Frederick, making their way towards them.

Byron broke the contact a good minute before he really needed to, and Hayley felt the significant drag of every second until the patient and the SES team arrived.

CHAPTER NINE

BYRON arrived at a quarter past eight the following Thursday evening, when Max was safely asleep. Hayley was already on edge. Chris had phoned a few days previously, announcing a plan to come for a three-day weekend. 'I should get there Friday,' he'd told her.

'Morning or afternoon?'

'Not sure. A bit flexible at the moment. Depends on what I arrange with my classes. I'll just turn up, OK? I'm really looking forward to it.' His voice had been soft, caressing.

His phone call left her with the usual uneasy feelings of worry about his safety, as well as a new sense of conflict. If they were going to make a serious attempt at rekindling their marriage, it had to be now or never. She couldn't keep going like this.

Byron had given her a living-in-the-moment passion that she knew she wouldn't find with Chris, but Byron had nothing to offer her future. Chris did. He offered a future that would give Max a father and herself at least a chance at contentment and security. It was something to work on. It would give her personal life a pattern and a shape. It would banish day-to-day loneliness.

At the moment, those things seemed very arid, compared to the way her heart immediately started

pounding when she heard Byron's car in the driveway. Was she just being a fool?

Since she was still uncertain about the undercur-
rents between them on the weekend, in the aftermath
of that dramatic rescue at Robson's Point, she forced
herself to stay in the kitchen until he'd rung the bell,
and then went to answer the front door with a teeth-
gritted determination not to hurry. Playing hard to
get? Who was she fooling? She was rewarded for her
trouble by the sight of a complete stranger.

No, on second glance it was definitely Byron, but
this was B.J. Black as she'd never seen him before.

He wore a black dinner suit with a white shirt and
black silk tie, and he was lazing in the doorway like
Cary Grant in an Audrey Hepburn film. He had a red
rosebud in his buttonhole and a dozen more—long
stemmed, glossy leaved, dark crimson, offset by
baby's breath and camellia leaves—in an extravagant
bouquet dangling casually from one hand. He was
grinning with studied intent.

'You wanted trimmings, Hayley,' he said, in a
voice that was tinged with dangerous meaning. 'And
I undertook to provide them.'

'I… Yes. Come in.' She took the roses, hands fluttering and heart skipping several beats. The thought
of protest didn't even enter her mind. There simply
wasn't room. 'Thank you. These are just beautiful.'

'I have more in the car.'

'More roses?'

'Other things. Also falling, I hope, under the defi-
nition of trimmings.'

'Byron, I told you the other day, you didn't
have to—'

'Oh, yes! I had to. You were right. This stuff is important, too.' The intent was even stronger, dark and syrupy and hot. 'And I'm going to enjoy every second of it. You take care of the roses, while I get everything else.'

She was too flustered to treat the beautiful blooms with the dignity they deserved. Instead, she grabbed the only vase she possessed that was big enough to hold them. She filled it almost to overflowing with tap water, clumsily removed the elegant Cellophane wrapping, with its huge bow, and stuffed the long stems into the water, which slopped all over the bench-top. Despite the cavalier treatment, the flowers still looked fantastic, set on the polished rosewood sideboard she'd inherited from her grandmother.

Byron was back, and as soon as she saw that suit again—it looked good enough on him to melt her knees completely—she blurted aloud, 'I'll have to change.'

He raised a deliberately sardonic eyebrow, then swept his glance down her figure and up again. 'I'll look forward to the result.' She pressed hot palms to hotter cheeks, whirled around and fled the room, chased by the sound of his softly teasing laughter.

Her wardrobe was suddenly, yawningly empty. This floral thing? Heavens, no! Her bridesmaid's dress from Melanie's wedding eight years ago? Why did she still have that? In the end, since they weren't actually leaving the privacy of the house, she resorted to a black silk slip which didn't fully cover the black lace bra beneath and a slinky Lycra-blend black jacket that she'd bought on impulse last year and never worn.

She put on make-up and heels, brushed her hair until it fluffed around her face, found her dangliest gold earrings and emerged breathless, aware that she had been absent for far too long.

He didn't seem to mind. And he had been busy.

There was a cream linen cloth on the coffee-table now and two tall crimson candles, freshly lit. A picnic supper of delicate canapés and petits fours was set out on black stoneware plates, and champagne flutes awaited filling. He was fiddling with something on the sideboard beside the roses, and when some quavery and scratchy sounds filled the air, she realised it was an antique gramophone. She recognised the smoky, passionate voice of Edith Piaf.

Byron reached for the champagne, and Hayley watched him deftly extract the cork and tip the bubbling, pale gold liquid into the glasses. A thread of vapour smoked for a second or two, then disappeared, and the air suddenly smelled sweet.

Hayley couldn't speak. Byron lifted the glasses and handed one to her, letting his fingers brush across hers. They sipped and then kissed, the sweetness and the bubbles mingling in their mouths.

'Where did you get the gramophone?' Hayley asked him.

'It's wonderful, isn't it?' he agreed. 'Believe it or not, Dad just never threw it out. He was a bit of a hoarder, and I helped Mum go through his shed after he died.' He laughed, and Hayley could see the memories flooding his mind. 'You know, Mum would send him off to the dump with a load of junk she'd culled from around the house. Little did she suspect that half of it never made it beyond that shed of his.'

'Was it hard when you had to go through it all?'

'It was, and it wasn't,' he said, after some thought. She loved the way his voice dropped to a lower and more resonant pitch when he spoke seriously like this. 'We got some good laughs out of it, and a few tears. Mum railed at him, beyond the grave, for putting her through it but in a way I think it helped. Both of us. I wasn't the only one who seized on some of the things we found as long-lost treasures.'

'It would have been a lot harder if she hadn't had you there to help.'

'Well, that goes for everything in life, doesn't it?' he answered. 'Human beings aren't cut out for too much solitude, especially not in all those elemental events like birth and death. In our hearts, don't most of us stay as social as preschoolers?'

She laughed. 'You're not wrong about preschoolers! Max isn't livable without having a friend over these days. I'm made well aware of what a poor substitute I am.'

'I expect you still have a small role to play!'

'Yes, I'm useful for hugs and treats and stories, and kissing scrapes better.'

'Speaking of scrapes, I got some news on our casualties from the other day.'

'Oh, yes, I wanted to hear. I read the newspaper report, but that said less than I knew already.'

'Well, our second fisherman, the one who held his unconscious mate in the water, was fine, as we were sure he would be. Just one night in hospital. The other two have both recovered consciousness, though the one who was airlifted from the water was a little slow and still has some loss of function.'

'That's so much better than it could have been.'

'I know. The other man's leg was badly shattered, and he did have a lacerated spleen, as we suspected. Our eye witness, Colin Frederick, is in a below the knee cast, out of hospital and doing fine.'

His face softened suddenly.

'You look beautiful, by the way,' he said, and leaned to brush one swift, studied and searing kiss across her mouth.

She arched her neck at once, eager for more. It felt like far too long since she'd been in his arms. Her whole body had reacted already.

'You were right, Hayley,' he whispered. 'Trimmings are important. I shouldn't have underestimated them as essential ingredients in an affair. It was my fault.'

'Stop apologising,' she said huskily.

Their kiss lasted for ages, but she couldn't surrender to it as she wanted to. This whole scene—the thought he'd put into it, the detail—should have had her swooning like a Regency virgin. Instead, it felt like just what he'd labelled it.

Essential ingredients in an affair.

And I don't want an affair. I'm in love with him. I want everything.

Framing the words in her mind like silent heartstricken cries, she knew she'd felt this way almost from the beginning, and that she'd been a coward not to let herself see it before this. She'd fallen in love with him so fast. She couldn't have done anything else.

Easy as falling off a log. Easy as the puzzles she helped Max with at preschool. Because, just as with the puzzles, she'd had all the pieces already at hand. Trust, respect and understanding. Shared interests, shared concerns, shared history. And finally a chemistry so strong that it had to last, if not for ever then as long as any human being could ever hope for.

Easy. Like the way they made love right there on the couch, surrounded by the remnants of their perfect supper, while her mind buzzed with stark new understanding.

Easy?

Falling in love with him had been easy. Living with how she felt was going to be much, much harder.

A man shouldn't have to do this at thirty-four, Byron thought as he drove away down Hayley's darkened street, hours later.

This sort of furtive sneaking away at the lowest ebb of the night should be the exclusive province of those on the very cusp of adulthood. He himself, in fact, had never had to do it at all. He and Elizabeth had both been living in mixed-gender student accommodation during the early days of their relationship, and their comings and goings had been no one's business but their own. Easy. No need for subterfuge. He'd liked it that way.

Sneaking home to bed and hoping that Robyn's sister, Simone, wouldn't notice quite how late he'd come in just wasn't his style, and it left him with a nagging sense that something was missing…wrong. He didn't want to be doing this. It seemed to dishonour Hayley somehow, and she didn't deserve that.

In contrast, he'd been…satisfied with his extravagant delivery of Hayley's desired 'trimmings' tonight.

Sophisticated men had known down the ages that an affair could be kept in its proper place by flowers and champagne administered at strategic intervals.

Handling the evening in just this way damped down his growing sense of restlessness and unease. It was all right. He wasn't getting out of his depth with this. He wasn't in danger.

Love doesn't come twice. I've been lucky. I've had it. It's gone.

The familiar creed loomed in his mind like a smooth rock in a stormy sea—something safe to cling to. Since he wouldn't love that way again, there was no risk of loss. And with Chris on the scene, Hayley was safe, too.

Chris was planning a visit soon, she'd told Byron tonight. She'd sounded self-conscious, a little clumsy. If she could rekindle her marriage, it would be the best solution for everyone.

Definitely.

Byron's body felt stiff and creaky and cold as he went up his front steps. The key rattled in the lock instead of gliding in and turning smoothly, and he was fairly certain that Simone would have woken at the sound. Damn!

Wearily, and purely for the sake of appearances, he reached his room, stripped to his underwear and climbed into bed. Pain kicked in his stomach and he had a bitter suspicion that most of what he'd told himself tonight was totally wrong.

'Where are you, Chris?'

'In Melbourne, of course.'

'You haven't left yet?'

'I'm not coming, Hayl. Sorry, it's short notice, but a contact who runs a self-defence school about twenty minutes from mine has asked me to take his classes this weekend, and I kind of feel it's a good opportunity.'

'Not to poach his students?'

'No! Geez, Hayley!'

'Sorry,' she apologised automatically. She thought, yes, I do automatically assume the worst. He's right. I shouldn't. Yet hasn't he given me enough reason to, over the years?

'I mean combining our schools,' Chris was saying. 'It'd reduce our admin costs and we could advertise more effectively.'

'That sounds like a good strategy. If you're sure the two of you could work together.'

'Well, obviously, yeah, that's what we'd need to talk through. Our expectations. Would you mind if I run the whole thing past you when it's worked out?'

'No, of course not.'

'You keep my feet on the ground, Hayl. I appreciate that. I need it.'

His voice caressed her. It set her teeth on edge. Panicked her, too, and she was shocked at her reaction.

He's serious about getting back together.

'Anyway, I'll try to make it in a couple of weeks instead. If that works for you.'

'Yeah, OK.'

She heard the thin note in her own voice.

And I don't want to. There's going to be a scene.

'It should be fine,' she went on vaguely. 'Max will be disappointed.'

'Two weeks isn't long.'

'No…'

Hayley put down the phone with a shaking hand. Two weeks. He was right. It wasn't long. And in two weeks, when he wanted to talk about their future, she knew she was going to turn her back on what he could promise, for the sake of a man who'd told her straight out he could promise nothing at all.

She looked at the clock. It was noon, nearly time to go and pick up Max from preschool. She had about twenty minutes in which to put away the groceries she'd shopped for, get a load of laundry onto the line…and come to grips with her life.

She felt a terrible, powerful urge to see Byron, talk to him, spill her heart's blood to him.

I love you. In comparison, what I feel for Chris is so thin. But at least it has a future. Being with you, I've tasted a sumptuous feast. Am I wrong to choose starvation now because Chris is only offering bread and water? Oh, Lord, if this is what it was like with you and Elizabeth, no wonder you're so sure you'll never find it again!

Her hand actually crept to the phone, and her head drummed with words. But she knew what a horrible mistake it would be. He mustn't guess how she felt. He'd be horrified! Guilty. Empathetic. She'd hate all of that.

Instead, she went to the kitchen. Put ice cream in the freezer, rice in the pantry, detergent under the sink. Just went on with her life. Byron had been doing it for four years, which proved it was possible.

She went out to the washing line at the far end of the garden with a heavy basket of wet clothes.

T-shirts, pyjamas, underwear... No more time. Grab the keys and jump in the car. Think of Max's funny little face lighting up as usual when he sees me. Try and make that enough of a reason to get up in the morning. Like Byron does. No wonder... No wonder all he wants is an affair.

The world came into focus again as Hayley parked the car, and she realised she'd driven here on a sort of autopilot. Preschool was its familiar self, sunny and bright, with the sounds of engines stopping and vehicle doors banging in the car park as other parents arrived.

One of them was Byron.

His smile caught her gaze at once. I'm thinking about last night, it said. That would have been enough to make her heart sing a few weeks ago, but it wasn't enough any more.

She blushed and let her eyes drop, too disturbed and upset to simply give him the answering yes-me-too smile that he was probably looking for. He looked incredible today, moving his big, virile body with a combination of carelessness and zest that should have been impossible but somehow, with Byron, *wasn't*.

His hair had grown since she'd first seen him again in February, she registered. It was heavy and thick on the top of his head today, and sculpted by the sea breeze into untidy waves. A closer look told her that it was a little damp. He must have taken a dip in the surf this morning.

She took a deep breath.

'How was the water?'

He put a hand to his hair. 'You noticed.'

'Only because I know how it looks—and feels—

when it's dry.' Painfully honest, but he didn't take it that way. He thought she was flirting.

He grinned, and her heart flipped up into her throat.

They walked side by side up to the preschool veranda, each saying nothing, while clusters of mothers and a couple of other dads chatted about local events. The children weren't ready to come out yet, still intent on the story that Karen was reading to them.

Byron stepped closer to Hayley and spoke quietly. 'You've got a night shift on Monday, right?'

'Yes.' She was surprised her voice still worked at all. Made the words as practical and plain as possible. 'With day shifts on the weekend, another night on Tuesday, and then I'm off until Sunday.'

'I'm taking Tori to Brisbane on Tuesday. I have a conference on Thursday and Friday, and we'll fly back Sunday morning. I'm working all this weekend, but I was wondering if you and Max would like to come for lunch on Monday.'

'I start work at six,' she said.

'I know,' he answered.

'OK, then…' she agreed carefully. 'When should we come over?'

'Any time. Eleven? Stay until you have to drop Max at your parents' house.'

His fingers brushed her hand secretly, out of sight of the other parents, and she shivered inside. Took her hand away only when Karen opened the sliding doors to welcome the parents in.

The weekend was…strange. It was like Byron's description of helping his mother clear out his father's shed after John Black's death. Hayley was tidying away the final remnants of her marriage. Not the actual, physical things like Chris's old roller blades and other sporting gear still cluttering her garage, but the mental things, the emotional things.

There were boxes in her mind with labels like 'The good memories' and 'Do I want to be a single mother for the next fifteen years?' which she had to sort through.

OK, this memory I'll keep where it is. This one, I think I was kidding myself, and I'd better move it to the bad memory box.

The 'single mother' box was a real mess, cluttered and overflowing with things like 'Reasons to get back together for Max's sake' and 'Fears about what will happen as Mum and Dad get older'. As if they were pieces of old, folded linen, she held each one up to the light of her current feelings and examined it, metaphorically, for holes.

The getting-back-together-for-Max's-sake idea turned out to be nothing *but* holes.

How could I ever have thought it was possible? How could I have thought that there was *ever* enough love, let alone that there was enough love still left?

She cried on Friday night, and on Saturday night. For Byron and the love of his life, which wasn't *her*. For herself and Chris, who hadn't ever known how that felt.

On Sunday, at work, she brought two heroin addicts back from the brink of death with injections of an anti-narcotic drug. She and Alison brought the first addict to hospital because he was in such bad shape, but the second just yelled abuse at them for destroying his hit then fled the scene.

They didn't see as many overdoses in Arden as they would have in a major city, but Hayley knew the routine all the same. So did Byron, whom she encountered at the hospital a short while later.

'You've got a red mark on your cheek,' he said. 'I take it the absconder wasn't grateful that you'd saved his life.'

'Apparently not!'

'You OK?'

'I'm fine,' she said, although it wasn't quite true. 'Looking forward to tomorrow.'

'Same here.'

The day came after a sound sleep on Sunday night and a sleep-in the next morning while Max watched some children's shows on television. He was pleased about going to play at Tori's.

'I like her. She's good at climbing and building sand castles,' he told Hayley in the car.

'We'll probably go to the beach, since it's just across from her house,' Hayley answered. 'So you'll get to play in sand with her then.'

'I'm going to make drippy castles.' Which was one of their own favourite pastimes on the beach, letting watery sand run between their fingers to create fantastical pointed castles like turrets of melted candle wax.

Until lunchtime, however, the children played at the house. It was a few weeks since Hayley had been here, and the lawn was fully grown now. It softened the atmosphere of the dramatic architecture, as did various pieces of furniture and craft items which Byron was gradually adding to his stunning home.

He was still at work in the garden when they arrived, putting vivid New Guinea impatiens into big glazed pots along a shady south-facing wall. Meanwhile, the children had immediately raced off into Tori's room, from where Hayley soon heard the rattling sound of a big box of Lego being dumped onto the floor.

'I remember those paint-stained jeans,' she teased him with an effort, after he'd showed her his morning's work.

'I won't offer to let you give them the same treatment you gave them before,' he answered.

'Peeling them off you in the shower? I should think not!'

She grinned at him, feeling her tension dissipate. She loved him, and she was with him, and he was gazing at her with desire in his eyes. Maybe it was enough.

'Or pelting them with mud, along with the rest of me. Come here,' he ordered gruffly, and she went willingly into his arms. 'Do you know how often I think about that night?' he said, the words tangled with his kiss.

'As often as I do, I hope,' she answered.

The rest of the universe faded into insignificance as they held each other, and desire pooled hot and heavy and low inside her. It was several minutes before he pulled away. They smiled uncertainly at each other, turned away at the same time and didn't say anything more about it. Surely that wasn't fear she'd seen in his eyes?

'Would you like coffee or something?' he asked vaguely, and she said yes just to give them both something to do.

The children's announcement that they were hungry was a welcome one, although a little early at half past eleven. Byron had the makings for some hearty sandwiches, and they'd all eaten by just after noon.

'Beach?' he suggested as they cleared up the kitchen together.

'Max is hoping to. He told me in an approving tone that Tori is very good at playing in sand.'

'She learned from a master. I'm very good at it, too.'

'You realise I'm not going to take that on trust.'

'I'll be happy to prove it to you.'

It was lovely on the beach. The breeze was mild and the sun was bright. Winter down here was usually confined to just one month of the year, and that month—July—was still a while away. Many people swam or surfed all year round.

Hayley put on her one-piece navy and white swimsuit with a T-shirt on top, and dressed Max in a similar fashion. Tori had a frilly pink and mauve 'sea shirt' made of a special sun-block fabric to cover the scarred area of her burns, and they all wore hats which blew off every time the breeze freshened.

The sand was cool beneath Hayley's feet and between her toes, and she was happy to watch as Byron created a fabulous sand kingdom with the children's help. Well, she was always happy to watch him, wasn't she? He made castles and moats, tunnels and highways, a hole that filled itself with seeping sea water for little feet to splash in, and decorative motifs of shells and seaweed on all major public buildings.

His energy was pure and contagious, and it was one of the things she loved about him, a quality she'd seen in him sixteen years ago that hadn't changed. This was *grounded*, this love. No doubt at all that it was real. She knew him too well for illusions.

'OK, now dig from your end, Max,' he said, 'and we'll meet in the middle.'

'I am digging, but I'm not getting there.'

'You will. Just keep going. There! Feel my fingers?'

Max giggled as their two sets of damp, messy fingers met beneath a solid bridge of sand. 'Can we make it wider, Daddy?' he said, then giggled again. 'Oops, I called you the wrong thing. Mummy, I called him Daddy—wasn't I silly?'

He looked towards her for the confirmation of an answering laugh, but Hayley couldn't do it. Couldn't make it come. It would have sounded as rusty as blunt shears sawing through an old can. Oh, Lord, it had just been a child's easy mistake on Max's part, a slip of the tongue, but still she couldn't laugh because it was so exactly what she wanted.

Byron had glanced at her, too, and she rushed to down play the moment. Didn't want Tori to comment in her bright, confident way. Didn't want anyone— especially herself—to go on thinking about it.

'Very silly,' she answered her son. 'The same way that you call me Grandma sometimes when you're not thinking.'

She held her breath. Max said, 'Yes!' And laughed again.

A moment later, they'd all gone back to what really counted—the elaborate sand creation. Tori was searching for more shells.

'Can you help me find them, Hayley?' she asked easily.

'Of course I can, love. They're so pretty, aren't they?'

'My favourites are the pink and white ones.'

'I can't decide. I like them all. Look at the tiny zigzag patterns on these ones.'

Max had decided to build a wall of seaweed so big and strong that no tide could possibly wash their work away. Byron was using a toy tractor to bulldoze a new highway across the bridge he and Max had created. Picking up handfuls of tiny, pointed shells with intricate patterns of stripes in pink and brown and tan and white, Hayley knew she was probably the only one who was still thinking about her son's innocent slip.

She thought about it as she watched Byron's energy and pleasure, and the children's confidence and joy. She thought about it as his dark head bent close to Tori's fair one, and as Max casually climbed across his extended, sandy legs to reach his seaweed wall.

This is what I want. I want my son to think of this man as a father. I want us to be a family. And I know I'll never have it, so how hard will it be to keep going this way?

To be happy with just the things they already had. Sex and friendship, rationed according to babysitting hours, and limited to days off.

'Tori, little mate, don't— Ah, too late!' Byron said.

'Oops!' With her small fists full of shells, she'd just trodden right in the middle of Max's sand bridge, which had collapsed beneath her weight.

Max wasn't pleased. 'Tori, you did that on purpose!'

'No, I didn't.'

'Yes, you did, and now I'm going to wreck your castle!' He moved towards it in a purposeful way, and Hayley had to intervene quickly before the whole thing escalated into fighting and tears.

'Maybe a walk?' Byron suggested, across the tops of two defiantly angled heads.

'Definitely a walk!' Hayley agreed. 'Let's play wave chasey, guys!' she suggested in a bright tone to the kids, before they could decide that a walk wasn't nearly as much fun as wilfully destroying each other's creations.

'What's wave chasey?' Tori asked.

'It's when we skip along the beach, just out of reach of the water, and anyone who gets caught by a wave has to...' Her mind blanked, but Byron came to the rescue.

'Turn a cartwheel or a somersault,' he said.

This apparently was a more fun idea than destroying sand landscapes, because both four-year-olds jumped up and started the game with lots of laughter and shrieking while Hayley and Byron were still debating whether to bring towels and hats.

When they finally got going, with towels but no hats, Byron growled at her, 'You had to say "skip", didn't you? Not "walk" or "jog" but "skip".'

'Skipping is the fun part. You have to skip.'

'I don't. You can.'

'I'm going to!'

Byron loped along behind while Hayley skittered

wildly across the sand to catch up to the children, just as emotion caught up to her.

I can't. I can't keep going like this, knowing I'll never want to end it, so that I'm just waiting for the moment when he does.

Affairs ended. Relationships in which—very carefully and openly—no promises were made *ended*. Ultimately, nothing counted without promises. That was why even Byron's delectable 'trimmings' the other night had left her ultimately unsatisfied. They'd added distance, they hadn't taken it away, and she somehow knew that he was glad about that. He'd done it deliberately, giving flowers and champagne with one hand, taking away the deepening of intimacy with the other.

No promises, and she *wanted* promises—the same promises that Chris had once made but had been unable to fulfill. The promises that Byron had made to just one woman in his life and had told Hayley he'd never be able to make again.

She felt a sick welling of jealousy for Tori's lost mother and Byron's lost love that horrified her and set her heart thudding painfully against her ribs.

I can't let myself feel this way.

Unfortunately, it wasn't something you could extinguish at will, like the candles on a birthday cake.

'You OK?'

He had caught up to her, and she realised it was because she'd unconsciously slowed, striding through the foamy reaches of the waves without even feeling the cold against her calves and feet.

'Just…thinking a bit.'

He was silent for a moment, then said carefully,

'How did it go this weekend with Chris? You haven't said anything.'

'He cancelled at the last minute. Something else came up. Something good, actually. He may be going into partnership with another small self-defence school. He's thinking so much more practically about the future these days.'

She heard the implication in her words—their personal future, as well as the future of his business—and held her breath, desperately hoping Byron wouldn't pick up on it.

Don't ask. Just don't ask.

She wouldn't be able to lie to him. If he asked straight out, she'd have to tell him the truth.

No, there's no chance we'll be getting back together.

But if Byron thought there was, it offered her a small protection, it bought her a little time in which to work out what she had to do.

Please, don't ask.

She didn't say it aloud, but her face must have said it for her because Byron didn't, just matched his stride to hers and splashed along beside her. The children turned and saw them, and Tori shrieked, 'A wave got you! Daddy *and* Hayley. You're wet all over your legs! You have to do cartwheels!'

'Yep, we do,' Hayley agreed.

She ran up the beach out of reach of the water and turned three in quick succession.

'Will a handstand do?' Byron asked.

Max yelled, 'Yes! A handstand! But only if you stay up for ages!'

'Here goes, then.'

He staggered along on his hands for several metres, while Hayley and the two children clapped and cheered, then he tipped back onto his feet, grinning. Hayley couldn't tear her gaze away.

His chest was bare and smooth and strong, his hands were coated in sand and his navy blue board shorts were a little faded and stained with salt. He looked happy and confident and rather wild, and she wanted so badly to belong in his life.

So badly. But it wasn't going to happen.

Should she hang on to what they had, while waiting all the time for the axe to fall, or should she get out now, before he guessed and the imbalance between them made even clandestine love-making and child-oriented friendship impossible?

'Did he say when he'd next try to get here?' Byron asked.

For Hayley, the question came out of the blue and she had to blink and reorient herself—oh, of course, Chris—before she understood and could answer. Waiting for her reply, Byron frowned.

'He's… It's OK,' she managed finally. 'He's going to try and get here in a week or two.'

'Not so long to wait.'

'No.' She groped in her mind for something more to say, and finally blurted, 'Max just shrugged when I told him. Should I hate that? Or should I be thankful? That this is all he knows about what having a father is like?'

'He knows there are other kinds of fathers. Your dad. Me, perhaps.'

'Yes.' She nodded tightly. 'There's you.'

All at once, she just couldn't talk about any of it any more, and turned away from him to follow the scampering children along the beach.

CHAPTER TEN

BYRON'S expectations regarding the trip to Brisbane had been mainly on Tori's behalf. He wanted her to stay as close as possible to Elizabeth's parents and brothers. Tori had four Galloway cousins living there, whom she deserved to know better. He also wanted to spend some good time with her himself, away from the stresses of their regular routine.

He planned to attend only the most relevant conference sessions, deliver his own short paper and turn up at the formal dinner on Friday night. The stuff around the edges he could skip, in favour of sitting by Monica's and Alan's solar-heated pool, watching Tori splashing around with her Floaties on.

That part turned out to be much more rewarding and restorative for Byron than he had expected. He realised that he was the one, not Tori, who had been stressed by things at home lately. Getting the house finished, settling into the job, Tori's burns, his ongoing concern over his mother's health, although she was progressing well now and managing comfortably with his aunt's and uncle's help at home.

How long was it truly, however, since he'd taken a proper break?

Not since before Tori was born.

Dear heaven, could that be true? He examined the idea more closely and found that it was. With the dark monster of grief looming behind him, he'd been

194

afraid to stop in case it caught up and he was over-
whelmed. He'd gone straight back to work after
Elizabeth's death, with a small baby to look after in
every spare moment. He hadn't let himself relax for
a single day.

He'd felt Monica in his life as the loving and sup-
portive presence she was, and yet, he now saw, he'd
been inhibited by her, too. He hadn't wanted to risk
hurting her by…this was strange…really living, starting to live again, when her only daughter was dead.

It had been him. Monica hadn't been putting it on
him. She wouldn't have. He had been setting those
limits on himself…

As he'd envisaged when planning this trip, he and
Monica were sitting by the pool, watching Tori swim,
while they sipped tea and ate fruit cake. Even in early
May, the weather was warm enough to penetrate
bone-deep, and the Galloways' lush tropical garden
was alive with flowers and birds.

'Darling, don't take off the Floaties!' Monica
called to Tori.

'I want to see if I can swim.'

'Wait till one of us is in the pool with you.'

'OK, then, I'm coming out now. I'm going on the
swing.'

'All right, sweetheart,' Byron said, then added
abruptly to his mother-in-law, 'When you moved up
here, how much of it was because of me?'

She looked at him in silence for a moment, then
said, 'Are you looking for an actual percentage figure?'

'Not really,' he conceded. 'I suppose I'm just looking for acknowledgement, so that I can thank you for

it. It was…perceptive of you, and generous, to realise that I needed to be on my own.'

'Some people would have said I was leaving you in the lurch.'

'I felt a bit that way at first. But I can see now that it was necessary.'

'For me, too, B.J. It would have been hard for me to have a front row seat on a daily basis while you were falling in love again, although, believe me, I do want that for you, very sincerely.'

What?

'Don't want it for me, Monica,' he said quickly. 'I can't see it happening. I'm not looking for it.'

'Does that mean…? Aren't you…still seeing Wendy?' she asked carefully.

He blinked. Wendy already seemed so long ago, although it was only six or seven weeks since he'd last asked her out.

'No, I'm not,' he said briefly. 'I probably should have told you that while you were staying with us, since it was examining my reaction to the two of you in conversation together which convinced me I wasn't ready, and that I didn't want to be.'

'Not ready? Oh, Byron, I think you're more than ready, and I wish you *did* want to be. I just didn't particularly like the idea of having Wendy as a daughter-in-law, that's all. You know I'll regard her—whoever she is, whenever she is—as a daughter-in-law, don't you?'

He saw the appeal and the yearning in her face and knew that, despite the generosity in what she was saying to him, she still grieved.

'I'd be honoured if you would,' he said, and a vivid

picture came to him of Hayley and Monica sitting and talking together by this very pool. Monica would warm to Hayley very strongly, he was sure.

Wait a minute...

'Only,' he added firmly, 'the situation isn't likely to arise.'

He shook his head as if to clear sea-water from his ears, and felt a lancing pain inside him that didn't make sense. He had exactly the relationship he wanted with Hayley, didn't he? The relationship he'd chosen. The only relationship he was capable of.

And yet he missed her horribly, far more than he'd expected to. Memories and images of the time they'd spent together ambushed him constantly, bringing a grin of appreciation or a stirring of desire. He was already kicking himself for not arranging when he'd next see her, so that he had something to look forward to. It had been a long time since he'd looked forward. Looking *back* was what he knew best.

But Monica was speaking again, very carefully.

'What is it that you believe, Byron? That you and Elizabeth were so perfect for each other that you could never love another woman as much? That's not true!'

'Isn't it?' he queried scratchily.

'No! You were, both of you, good at love, that's all. Good at the kind of love that marriage requires. Some people just are, and being able to love in that way is a talent like any other. It doesn't abandon you. It's not tied to one person. You'll find another woman to love in that way one day.'

'What if I don't want to?' he said rebelliously, his

voice only barely controlled. 'What if the prospect of loss just scares me too much?'

'Of course it'll scare you, B.J.,' Monica answered. 'That prospect is always frightening when we love deeply, whether it's our love for a child, or a parent, or even a pet! But I think when it happens, you'll find that you don't have a choice.'

'Oh... Great! That's great!' His groan of sarcasm was shaky and he had his fingers pressed against his eyes.

'Yes, it *is* great. It's frightening, but it's still the greatest thing in the world,' Monica told him softly, and went to push Tori on the swing before he could open his mouth to strenuously argue back.

'Chris hasn't phoned you, has he, Mum?' Hayley asked, snatching a free moment at around four o'clock on Sunday afternoon.

She was working an eight till six day shift, and would be off in two hours. Things had been quiet so far.

'No, he hasn't,' Adele answered. 'Are you expecting to hear from him?'

'No, I'm expecting him to show up!' she retorted, on edge.

As usual, he'd been vague about it. 'Saturday or Sunday.' She'd taken this to mean Saturday night or Sunday morning, and had tried not to think about the fact that he was probably talking about another overnight drive.

She'd half expected him to show up for breakfast or ring from her mother's this morning to say he was taking Max off her hands for the day. Now, at four o'clock, came the first real concern. Why hadn't she heard?

She had been tense and unhappy all week as it was. Byron's absence since Tuesday had underlined just how strong her feelings for him had become. She *missed* him. It was heavy, constant and physical, and made her think, as she so often did, that if this was how he still felt about Elizabeth...

Without even the possibility of running into each other at the hospital or at preschool, let alone of spending any private time together, she was left only with her understanding of how empty the future would be when their affair inevitably ended...when she took her courage in her hands and ended it. Far emptier than it was now, with him and Tori merely away for a few days.

After putting down the phone, she chewed over Chris's silence...*stewed* over it...for another half-hour, growing increasingly on edge. Byron would be back from Queensland by now. She wanted to see him—it was a craving like hunger inside her—but she didn't know when she would. They hadn't made any plans.

The weekend was almost over. No overdoses. No alcohol-induced accidents. Just a couple of nice things. She and Lucas had brought a grateful diabetic back from a hypoglycaemic coma with one quick shot of dextrose. She'd delivered a baby, too, in a pretty, sun-filled bedroom on a little farm in the bush, because the healthy, three-and-a-half kilogram girl hadn't even wanted to wait as far as the back of the ambulance, let alone long enough for her labouring mother to get to Arden Hospital.

Finally, they'd told an elderly patient that he wasn't having a heart attack, according to their monitors and observations, and he'd believed them and had started feeling better and a whole lot more cheerful straight away.

But now Chris hadn't phoned, and his 'long weekend' was starting very late and she couldn't help feeling…damned angry, actually. She wasn't looking forward to hearing what he had to say, or to what she planned to say in reply. She wanted to get it over with!

When the phone did ring, with its ordinary rhythm and tone, not the special 'hotline' sound that signalled an emergency call-out, she snatched it up impatiently and gabbled, 'Arden Ambulance Station.' She wasn't even expecting it to be her ex-husband any more.

'Hayley?' Chris's voice.

'Where are you?'

'I got a late start. Sorry. I'll see you tonight.'

'Are you phoning from the car?'

'Yes.'

'*Where*, though?'

'From the car.'

'Yes, but—'

'See you later.' He rang off. The quality of the connection had been poor, and she resisted the need to try and phone him back.

It was irritating not to know when to expect him, or what time he'd left Melbourne, but she felt a wash of relief all the same. He was fine. On his way. And hopefully not tired, if he'd only left Melbourne after lunch. He'd be somewhere a few hours east of Melbourne by now, around Traralgon or Sale. He would probably show up at about ten, and she'd swallow her anger for Max's sake, and for the sake of the talking they needed to do, and accommodate whatever unreliable or unsuitable suggestions he made.

The phone stayed silent after Chris's call and she tried to keep busy with routine tasks around the station. Couldn't wait to hand over to the night crew today. She wanted to see Max and hug him extra close, for some reason.

Five-thirty, twenty-five to six, twenty to six. Right up until six, any call-outs were their responsibility, not that of the incoming crew, and it was only a quarter to six when the hotline sounded.

Hayley picked it up and heard a concise summary from the dispatcher. 'We have a vehicle off the road about twenty kilometres south of town,' he said. 'Doesn't sound too good. Going too fast, then braked hard on a bend. Caller saw it happen.'

'OK, we're out of here,' Hayley said, resigned more than anything else. You had to keep some emotional distance in this job in order to do it properly.

She drove, listening to a further report from the dispatcher over the ambulance radio. 'Single male occupant. Caller has advanced first-aid qualifications and a portable fire extinguisher, which he's used around the car as he could smell petrol. He says the driver is definitely injured, not fully conscious and probably trapped by the legs. I've talked to SouthCare, and there's a helicopter available. We have police on the scene now. They were patrolling in the area.'

'OK, traffic's pretty good,' Lucas radioed back. 'We should be seeing something soon. Yes, I can see

a police car up ahead.' He signed off, then whistled
as he and Hayley both saw the car. 'We're going to
be here for a while.'

Thank God for Mum and Dad, Hayley thought,
watching her evening with Max slide away. As yet,
she was hardly thinking of their patient.

The car looks familiar—that was her first vague
thought. It was a big green Holden, just like Chris's,
but it was facing south and it was off the left shoulder
of the highway, not the right. Heading towards
Melbourne, she assumed.

She took out the oxygen kit, the ECG pack, blood-
pressure cuff and drug kit, then heard one of the po-
licemen saying, 'Driver fatigue? Distracted on the
bend? This is the path the car took across the road.
It rolled at least once, hit the tree and ended up looking back the way it came.'

The way it came. From Melbourne. A big, green
Holden.

'Chris. Oh, my God, it's Chris!' She recognised the
patches of rust converter on the paintwork now. Chris
had never got around to respraying the old car in its
original green.

'Hayley?' Lucas's voice was higher than usual.

'It's my ex-husband,' she gasped.

'Oh, no!'

She tried to walk but her knees buckled, and Lucas
caught her in his arms to steady her. The equipment
they were both carrying pressed sharp corners into her
flesh. She was almost oblivious to the police and the
rescue crew, who had arrived now as well.

'Can you handle it?' Lucas asked, sounding shaky.
He was just a level one trainee, not legally permitted

to use advanced life-support techniques, even if he knew how.

She wanted to say, Yes, I can handle it, but the words wouldn't come. This felt too much like a dream, something she'd brought into being through her own fears, not something that had actually happened...was actually happening...to Max's father.

Finally, she croaked, 'Yes.' She only said it because she *had* to handle it, not because she was convinced that she could.

'I'll call for a second crew,' Lucas answered.

'Yes. Please,' she agreed automatically as her cotton-wool legs took their first few steps towards the crushed green car. 'He'll need a neck brace and backboard, Lucas. Possibly the MAST suit. What else? I can't think...'

She'd never worked in anything like such demanding and confronting circumstances. Fitting an oxygen mask to the face she'd once kissed with starry-eyed love, looking for a usable vein in arms that had held their newborn child, talking to him not as the professionally friendly and reassuringly competent paramedic she usually was but as his ex-wife.

'Chris, you're going to be fine, OK? It's Hayley. Can you talk to me? Can you open your eyes for me?'

He did it, dragging his flickering lids up with effort to reveal the familiar brown that had once so entranced her. The wash of relief at the sight of his reactive pupils didn't help her strength to return.

'Talk to me, Chris!'

Just a single sound, a groan. No words.

'Max did a painting for you on Friday,' she went

on. 'I wish you could see it. Now, you have to give me your arm, OK? I need to find a vein.'

She went on talking to him—'Where are those veins hiding today, hey?'—exultant about his opened eyes, even though he'd closed them again straight away, but above all *angry* with him. Oh, dear Lord, how she hated that! She'd been angry with patients before—ungrateful addicts, drunken drivers, people who called an ambulance when they required little more than an adhesive bandage or a headache tablet—but it hadn't been like this.

It was boiling inside her, *hurting* her every time she thought of Max, making her hands shake so that she knew she wouldn't be able to get a needle into those weakly pressured veins.

'Lucas!' she yelled. 'His BP's down. Eighty systolic. Pulse thready. But I can't get a vein... Do we have a second crew coming?'

'I've called for one. They had another call-out. I explained the situation. I don't know what the story is.'

She burned with pointless regret. If only this was Bruce working with her today, not Lucas! At his level, he wasn't even permitted to cannulate. She was sorely tempted to get him to try anyway. To hell with protocol! He'd seen it done enough times now. She could talk him through it. His hands would have to be steadier than hers. With these flat veins, though, the vital thing was experience.

I'm the one with the experience.

She tried again.

Failed.

Her hands felt as lifeless as the veins she was trying

to probe. Chris was moaning and mumbling now. She couldn't understand him, but tried to talk to him some more, squeezing herself farther into the cramped space of the passenger seat while strident noises signalled that the car was being cut to try and get to Chris's legs.

Her anger against her child's father ebbed in favour of anguish, and a new determination came.

'Chris, hang in there, OK?' Her voice strained painfully through her tense throat. 'I wish they'd learn to make that equipment quieter, hey?'

She *had* to do this! For Chris. For Max's father. For *Max*.

Her hands stopped shaking, she felt a rush of adrenalin and managed to get the drip into Chris's arm at last, pumping in the lifesaving blood substitute he needed. His blood pressure came up almost at once and he opened his eyes again.

'Hayley…' he said, then a minute later, with a wide, unfocused gaze, 'Is Max safe?'

'He's safe. He's fine. He's with Mum. You were on your own in the car, Chris,' she told him.

'I'm sorry. I can't remember what happened. I'm so sorry, Hayley…'

Then, incredibly, she heard Byron's voice behind her. 'Let me take over, Hayley. This isn't the best situation for either of you.'

'You're here,' she said vaguely, as if she must have conjured up his presence magically without even knowing it.

Twisting awkwardly in the cramped space, she felt his touch—an arm around her shoulder, a hand on her thigh. She closed her eyes for a long moment, just to

breathe him in. His warmth, and the scent of the sea
on his skin. The warmth and scent of the man she
loved.

'Second car at your station got called out to a
woman in prem. labour,' he answered her. 'Your dispatcher called the hospital—I got back early afternoon and came on at six—and said that this was…
well, that it was Chris. What's his status?'

Hayley's eyes snapped open again and she said
firmly, 'I'm handling it. It's OK.' She'd won that
huge battle for control when she'd cannulated the
vein. She was trained for this. She could do it.

'It's not,' he said. 'Hayley, you can't competently
treat a patient you're this close to.'

'I can. I have to. He's my ex-husband.'

'I know,' he said patiently. 'Which is why you
can't do it. Not now, when you don't have to. I'm an
emergency specialist, remember?'

Fight? Shall I go on fighting? came the distant
thought.

But the part of her that was still in control knew
that he was right, and she nodded to him in silence.

That same controlled part of her motivated her to
twist and slither from the car to let Byron take her
place. It pushed her to run through some figures on
Chris's condition, and outline to Byron what she'd
already done and what she suspected was wrong, then
she felt the last of the adrenalin drain from her system
to leave an after-shock of helplessness.

'You'll still need my input,' she asserted weakly.
But he simply shook his head and pushed her gently
away without even looking at her.

Someone put a blanket around her shoulders and

sat her in the back of the police car where she cried helplessly and prayed in a whisper, 'Don't let him die. Don't let my child's father die.'

She had no idea how much time had passed before Lucas appeared behind the open rear door of the police car.

'We're off,' he said.

'How is he?'

'Good. Conscious and lucid now. In a fair bit of pain.'

'Pain's…good,' she answered with an effort. That sounded wrong, but it was the truth. When a person was too seriously injured to feel the pain, then you really worried.

'Dr Black's going in the back of the car,' Lucas said. 'SouthCare's on its way. The police will bring you home.'

'No! I'm going in the car!'

She'd struggled out of the police car and was striding clumsily to the back of the ambulance before Lucas could react to stop her. Byron and Chris were already there. She climbed in, closed the big, familiar door behind her and sat on the little seat behind the driver.

Lucas activated lights and sirens and accelerated onto the highway seconds later. Hayley held Chris's hand, hardly aware of what Byron was doing, although she could have predicted it with her eyes closed if she'd thought about it.

Oxygen, ECG, blood pressure. Adjust the patient's fluids, give morphine for pain relief if his consciousness was good and his blood pressure was high enough.

Since there was good light in the back of the vehicle, Byron checked for signs of injury that they
might have missed on-site, in the darkness and
cramped conditions. Bruising to the chest, abdominal
tenderness or rigidity, limb injuries. He did a log roll,
looking for any evidence of spinal injury in the align-
ment of the vertebrae. She thought about asking what
he'd found, but couldn't frame the words, didn't want
to frighten Chris, who tended to get edgy when a lot
of medical language was bandied about.

His eyes had drifted shut, but she kept talking to
him quietly.

'You're going to Canberra, Chris. Max and I will
drive up first thing in the morning. I'm too shaky to
do it tonight. Max can bring you his paintings. Lots
of things. We'll put them up in your hospital room,
OK?'

Periodically, she wiped her eyes. On a tissue. On
the sleeve of her uniform shirt. On the blanket she
still had—though she didn't know why, she wasn't
cold!—around her shoulders.

I'm still crying, she thought distantly. For Max, and
for Chris, and because I don't want to be this angry…

She's a complete mess, Byron thought. He glanced
covertly across at her, saw the glistening wetness on
her face.

He had known that Hayley still had feelings for her
ex-husband. They'd talked about it. Chris had hinted
to Hayley that he wanted to have another try at their
marriage, and she was considering the idea. He'd
known all of that. Had actually *hidden* behind it for
a long time.

But it hadn't hit him until now just how strong and

unbrookable those feelings must actually be. Looking at her—at the stunned expression on her face, tracked by endless tears, the angular way she sat, the flaring emotion deep in her eyes—he felt a familiar wave of an ugly emotion whose name he knew well.

Jealousy. Envy. Hard to distinguish the two. Envy coupled with an impotent longing that deeply offended his habitual need to take action, to seek control over his own life. He'd known this feeling so many times after Elizabeth's death. Frequently he'd looked at other couples and felt this way.

They're happy. And I've lost her. And there's nothing in heaven or hell that I can do about it.

Raw and human and not very saintly, those feelings.

And different, he suddenly understood. Quite different to what he was feeling now. He wasn't envious of Hayley for her love for Chris. He was envious of Chris, because it was Chris whom Hayley loved.

And not me. She loves him and not me. I want her...I *need* her...to love me. The way I love her. Oh, dear Lord, I love her! What we've had together is only a fraction of what I want, and it's taken me this long to see it, to let go of the past, to realise that this is different but every bit as precious and real as what I found at eighteen. Monica was right. I didn't want it, it's frightening and painful, but it's happened—it happened ages ago—and there's nothing I can do about it!

So Hayley sat with tears streaming down her cheeks because of Chris. Chris himself was in a serious condition, with a crush injury to his legs and a probable lacerated liver. Byron himself fought to keep

his patient stable, wished deeply that he wasn't here,
and struggled against an absurd yet knife-sharp urge
to yell at the man, Prove yourself! She loves you.
You've let her down so many times. Make this accident at least make *sense*, by loving her back the way
she deserves! Tell her now! Squeeze her hand as hard
as you can and tell her!

Lucas gunned the heavy vehicle up the highway
with an iron grip on the wheel, yet from Byron's perspective he seemed to be crawling along. It was
amongst the longest few minutes of his life.

The SouthCare chopper was waiting on the helipad
beside the hospital, Hayley saw as they pulled in.

The transfer was completed without additional
problems. She watched the aircraft take off into the
night, gripped by a final irrational spurt of fear, and
faced the prospect of the drive up to Canberra with
dread. As soon as Chris was ready to hear it, she had
to tell him that he was too late. She couldn't go back
to their marriage. Longing to have the scene over
with, she knew it might be days or even weeks before
it could take place. Meanwhile, as she stood there, the
hospital staff who'd helped with the transfer drifted
back inside, and Lucas had already headed back to
the station. They both should have gone off duty ages
ago.

'Hayley...'

She felt Byron touch the small of her back. She
turned and stumbled instinctively into his arms. Their
contact was clumsy. She sought his comfort blindly,
but his arms were stiff, not nearly as giving and warm
as she needed them to be. How hopeless it all was!

After a moment, they both pulled away and stood with just their hands clasped loosely across a cool distance.

'I'm going to drive up tomorrow,' she said with an effort.

'I'll take you.'

'No… If it seems…too hard then Mum and Dad will come. Best if they do anyway,' she amended, struggling to think in practical terms. 'Max is too little to spend long at Chris's bedside. The hospital may not even let him visit at first. Thanks, though. Thanks for offering.' She brushed more tears away with the heel of her hand.

He didn't answer her directly. She wasn't even sure if he'd taken in what she'd said about her plans.

'I couldn't stand to see you crying like that in the ambulance,' he told her in a low, strain-filled voice instead. 'This will bring you closer. It'll work out for you. You've told me he wants it. You don't have to cry.'

'But I'm so angry with him,' she blurted out. '*So angry!*'

'It can happen when you really love someone. Love can encompass all of that at times like this.'

'I don't love Chris! I think I hate him at the moment. He knew the risks he was taking. Having been married to a paramedic, of all people, and not to listen to my warnings about speed and fatigue.' Her voice shook. 'I *didn't* nag! Not at first! But he ignored me. The man who phoned 000 said he was speeding. And he's Max's father, and if he'd killed himself today and left my precious, wonderful little boy without a dad…! Oh, dear God, I'm so *angry* with him!'

She felt Byron's sudden stillness, communicated through their joined hands. The balls of his thumbs were rubbing gently across her knuckles. Wind whipped across the helipad and blew through the inadequate thickness of her uniform shirt. Automatically, she'd left the blanket in the ambulance, where it belonged.

'Clarify something for me, Hayley,' Byron said slowly. Carefully. 'You're angry because he makes it hard for you to love him, right? And yet you still do love him.'

'Love him?' she echoed. The idea—it was the second time Byron had mentioned it—didn't make any sense at all. 'I— He's Max's father. At some level I'll always—I'll *try* to always love—no, care for him at least. Respect him as much as I can. But if you're asking me if I want him back... Why do you want to know this *now*?' She laughed jerkily. 'No, I don't want him back!'

Then she suddenly remembered that she'd been quite deliberately silent on the subject of late, letting Byron think it was still a possibility, purely out of self-protection. Too late for that cloak of protection now. She'd been too honest, and could only continue that way. She finished, 'I can't even imagine it now.'

He was silent, and she prompted, 'Byron?'

React, at least, to this betrayal of mine!

'I'm sorry,' he muttered, his gaze raking her face. 'I want to know *now*—which I admit is the worst possible timing—because I want it to mean...more than it can possibly mean.'

'You want me to love you.' She suddenly understood. 'Hell, you *want* me to feel like this?' She blinked back fresh tears. 'Is that fair, after all you've said about having nothing more to offer?'

Hayley looked up into his face, wanting so much to see it soften instead of looking so tight and hard to read. His dark eyes were black sea pebbles, washed by salt water. The seam of his lips was a slash of charcoal, made by a child's hand.

'I was wrong,' he answered simply at last. 'I do have more to offer. I didn't want it. I fought it all the way. But it happened anyway, and it's so wonderful that I'm not scared of it any more. I have *everything* to offer, Hayley, and I think you're about the only woman in the world who could have made me see that…and feel it…and hunger for it so much. Is it too late? I love you. I *love* you! Can I, please, change the terms of the agreement we made when we started this?'

Byron's arms were around her now, making a wide, warm cradle that was strong and sure and meant only for her. She ached to touch her mouth to his, to taste him again, to share the flaring heat of their response to each other, but she made herself wait. Made him wait, too. This was too important to get it wrong, to rush it, to misunderstand.

'The terms of the agreement,' she echoed softly, feeling her heart begin to race inside her chest. 'So how does it read now? Tell me, Byron.'

'I…uh…think I'd have to look it up,' he said. 'I believe there are numerous alternatives these days. We'd need to discuss the options.'

'Tell me the basic version. You know, we're big on protocol in the ambulance service.'

She was pretending, and he knew it. He could feel

how she was shaking, see in her eyes what she wanted him to say. And he said it.

'Hayley, I want you to marry me.' The words had all the passion and meaning she could have wanted. 'I don't care how we do it, or when. I want to live with you and have a baby with you, make plans with you, take holidays with you, learn to be a good father to Max in case Chris never really makes it work, and watch you becoming a mother to Tori—the only mother I could have found for her, because it had to be the woman who was right for me, too, and that's you. *Will* you?'

'Yes. Oh, yes. All of it,' Hayley answered him. 'All of it, Byron. I love you…'

She cupped his face between her hands and pulled his head down to meet her mouth, and his kiss was hungry, eager and achingly sweet. It felt like the only thing she'd ever truly wanted.

'What's that, love?' Hayley's mother said, pausing by a thick, cream envelope that lay on the counter-top in the big, modern kitchen.

'Oh, a wedding invitation, actually,' Hayley answered. 'It only came today, but we knew it was on the way. I hadn't told you, had I? Byron and I haven't decided whether we'll go. It's a no-children-allowed affair, so that would mean leaving Max and Tori with you.'

'You know that's not a problem if you really want to go. Byron's mother will help. She loves spending time with them, as long as there's another adult around for back-up.'

Mrs Black hadn't fully regained her mobility after the stroke.

'Well, yes, but it'll only be a couple of weeks before the baby is due, so I suspect we won't.'

Hayley laid a hand across her jutting stomach and felt a tiny answering kick. She was almost seven months pregnant now, and she and Byron were currently arguing, in a thoroughly enjoyable way, over names. They didn't know the baby's sex, so it was a battle on two fronts.

'But whose wedding, Hayley?' her mother persisted.

'Chris's.'

'Oh.'

'He met someone a bit over a year ago, when he was still having physio after the accident, and I could tell from the way he spoke about her that it was serious.'

'And he's asked you and Byron?' Mum sounded disbelieving and a little sceptical.

'I'm glad he did,' Hayley answered quietly. 'For Max's sake. It's far better if he knows that our lives are going on, we can be civil to each other and we're both happy.'

'And, of course, Max already knows that *you* are,' Adele said.

'He should!' Hayley blushed a little. 'Byron and I...uh...quite often find it difficult to keep the glow down to a respectable level around here.'

Comfortable arms came around her for a hug. 'I'm so glad, love! Not surprised, but very glad. Oh, is that Byron now?'

The sound of a car engine had floated up from the driveway.

'It should be,' Hayley said. 'He was picking up Max from soccer practice on the way home, and then Tori has Scottish dancing straight after dinner, which I'll take her to.'

At the moment Tori was doing some very complicated, important six-year-old girl thing in her room. They could hear her talking about it, all the way along the corridor, to no one in particular.

'She's gorgeous, Mum,' Hayley went on, lowering her voice. 'No evidence of dancing talent, but she loves it, which is all that matters. And I'm glad I stopped work early, because two six-year-olds in the same house make for a hectic lifestyle!'

'Wait until you have a new baby as well!'

They both listened as Byron and Max came up the front steps. The two came at once into the kitchen and family room, which had somehow become the heart of the house these days. Max was full of news straight away, along with a bone-crushing hug. He'd scored a goal at soccer. He had another wobbly tooth. He'd got a certificate for good work at school.

Giving Hayley barely enough time to reply, he turned and rushed off to his room.

Byron's entrance was just as eager, but less exuberantly and vocally expressed. His eyes connected with Hayley's across the room at once, as strong and focused as a beam of light, and his smile was that special one he only ever gave to her, suggesting a melody that only the two of them could hear.

Hayley would have liked a bone-crushing hug from him, too, but the little flare of heat in his eyes told her he was saving it for later, when they were alone. She'd get much more than a hug then.

They'd been married for nearly eighteen months now, and beyond everything else—beyond the chemistry and the friendship—it just felt right. It made sense of their lives, and of the past, in a way that nothing else ever could.

'Hello, B.J.,' Adele carrolled to him brightly.

She and Monica and Byron's mother—the three grandmothers-to-be—all got on extremely well, and she'd picked up the old nickname for her new son-in-law straight away. Hayley, who resisted it in favour of his full name, which she liked much better, put up with the fact graciously.

'Hi, Adele,' he answered. 'Staying?'

'No, just dropping in. If you're here, it's later than I think.' She glanced at the clock. 'Yes, it *is*. Quite a bit later!'

Byron's gaze fell on the envelope that sat on the counter-top, and Adele looked at it again, too.

'Quite a bit later...' she repeated absently, then added with sudden vigour, 'No, don't go.' Both other adults were confused. Wasn't she the one who was going? 'I've thought about it now. Take a holiday instead before the baby's born.'

'Can someone fill me in?' Byron said.

'Fill me in, too, Mum.'

'Don't go to Chris's wedding.'

'Oh, is that what this is?' Byron picked up the envelope and dropped it again straight away, without apparent interest.

'If you're going to leave the children with me— which I'd love—do it so that you can take a break

for yourselves. You haven't had one since the hon-
eymoon, and that was only three nights. It's your last
chance to get some time alone before the baby's born,
and you both push yourselves too hard.'

Byron and Hayley looked at each other. He smiled
that secret smile again and she stepped towards him
on feet that hardly touched the ground. 'Shall we?'
she said.

'Yes.' No hesitation.

'It doesn't matter where, does it?'

'Not at all. The point is to do it.'

'Yes,' she agreed.

They slid their arms around each other, their
mouths just an inch apart, and thought about it. No
one else. Just some quiet little place where they could
do nothing very much at all. Byron brushed a kiss
across her mouth, making the banked fire inside her
glow and flare. She wanted more, and parted her lips
to close them over his. Something kicked and rolled
low in her abdomen, and it wasn't the baby.

'Can't wait,' he murmured. 'Just can't wait...'

She dragged her mouth away, touched his face,
smiled at him, then turned aside.

'All right, Mum, yes, we'd love to...' she began.

But Adele was gone. They heard her in Tori's
room, saying goodbye to the children, so either she
must have tiptoed from the room or they'd been more
absorbed in each other than Hayley had thought.

The latter, evidently. There on the counter-top sat
the wedding invitation, ripped right through the middle with one firm tear, as if to announce, Now you
have no choice! They hadn't even heard the ripping
sound.

Byron picked the pieces up between fingers and thumbs and held them out, grinning. 'Did you need her to do this?'

'No. I was already quite convinced.'

'So was I,' he answered. 'So was I, my darling.'

He gathered her into his arms once more, and this time their kiss lasted much, much longer.

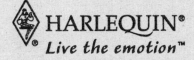

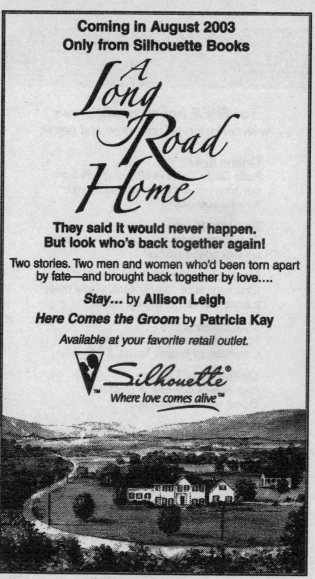

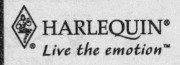